MW01232589

The
Other
Woman

Kim Corum

The Other Woman

New Tradition Books

The Other Woman
by
Kim Corum

New Tradition Books
ISBN 1932420045
All rights reserved

For information contact:
New Tradition Books
newtraditionbooks@yahoo.com

For Bert

Sit back, relax. And close your eyes.

This couldn't be happening.

My wife, Carrie, was kissing another woman! They were right there, right in front of my eyes, on the bed—on my bed!—sitting on their heels and staring at each other with undeniable intensity. I blinked. Yup. She was definitely kissing her. And I mean, really kissing her. She looked like she was going to do more. A lot more. They were so hot.

Carrie was a blonde and Veronica a brunette. A man couldn't ask for more. Both were undeniably gorgeous with hot little bodies.

Life couldn't get any better than this.

I watched with rapt attention as Carrie leaned over and brushed her lips against Veronica's. It looked like a nice kiss. She began softly at first, then with more passion. Her tongue gently probed Veronica's lips until they opened and allowed it inside her mouth.

Stuff like this never happened to me.

But they were kissing! They were actually doing it! I was as excited as a schoolboy with his first porn mag. No, I was way more excited than that.

Carrie kept kissing her and they fell back on the bed. Their hands began to explore the other's fully clothed body. Veronica's hands were now going up and down Carrie's back and then up under her shirt.

I was going to die.

They began to moan, almost in sync, as they moved against each other. They continued to kiss and the moans were getting louder. They were so hot they were sizzling. They were that into it. *Really* into it.

I moved closer to the bed. I didn't mean to, my dick just pointed me in that direction and I followed it. It wanted some attention too, but I hated to interrupt them. I really did. I could just stand and watch. I could watch forever. They wanted me to watch, they told me so. I wasn't going to do anything until they told me to. I wasn't going to screw this up. I was almost afraid they'd kick me out.

They began to tear each other's clothes off. A shirt came flying at me and landed on my head. I yanked it off and a skirt replaced it, then a pair of panties and then a bra. I dodged another skirt so I could see them unsnap their bras and wiggle out of them. Their lips stayed clamped together as they undressed. And then their bare breasts touched.

Only in my dreams had I seen anything like that. And in porno movies.

Carrie bent down and grabbed Veronica's tit. I watched in awe as her tongue came out and licked her nipple before she sucked it inside her mouth as she stared up at her. Her eyes were wide and beautiful. Veronica stared down at her and bit her bottom lip as if the feeling combined with the intensity of the situation was just too much to bear.

It was almost too much for me. I can honestly say that.

Carrie pulled back and licked it again, giving it a good, long stroke. Veronica grabbed Carrie's breast and clamped her mouth on it, sucked it until Carrie moaned and pulled her mouth back to hers and they kissed, rubbing and pressing their bodies against each other's deliciously. They moved hands and legs and didn't stop arching and moaning the whole time.

My dick was so hard it hurt.

Their hands stayed on one another's tits and rubbed deliciously. As if they loved touching and being touched at the same time. I loved the way their breasts rubbed against each other's. I wanted a touch or two myself. But, again, I didn't want to ruin the moment by being too greedy. Or too eager.

Carrie was now kissing her way down Veronica's naked body, biting at her skin. Veronica arched away from the bed and her bottom lip trembled as she glanced down at her. Carrie stared back and Veronica nodded and opened her legs wider.

Carrie's head went between her legs. A slight hiss came out of Veronica's mouth and she threw her head back and grunted. Carrie began to eat her, first using her tongue to slide up and down her wet pussy, and then she clamped her mouth onto it and sucked. Veronica let out a moan, this one more intense, and then she pushed Carrie away, pushed her back, turned around so her ass was facing me and got on top of her.

They were going to do a 69!

Carrie was now beneath Veronica and had her pussy in her face. Veronica's face was now buried in Carrie's pussy. Carrie moaned and began to move her pussy against Veronica's face. Veronica kept eating her, sucking at her as Carrie did the same. They used everything they had, their fingers and their noses and their tongues and mouths. They really seemed to enjoy doing it, too.

They kept at it for a little while and their pussies were all swollen and wet and looked so good. As they moved against each other and sucked and kissed and licked, they both began to come and I could tell they were coming because the kissing and sucking and licking got more intense and the moans got deeper, almost sounding painful. They began to rock, their bodies almost bucking against each other's. The moans grew into slight screams that ripped from their throats.

"Oh, GOD!" Veronica screamed. "OH GOOOD!"

"AHHHHHHHH!" Carrie screamed. "Oh baby! Oh baby!"

Baby? That's what she always called me. Huh.

"Don't stop, baby," she moaned. "OH! Don't stop!"

Yeah, don't stop.

Neither one of them stopped not until they were both spent. Carrie turned around and lay down next to Veronica and they cuddled and kissed a little, basking in that post sexual glow. Or maybe they were just waiting to get their strength back. I just stood there. I couldn't have moved if I had to. I almost didn't believe what had just happened. I know it did but it was almost too good to be true. How could it have just happened?

They were wrapped in each other's arms and looked quite cozy. Carrie stared over at me and a smile came to her lips. The corners turned up a little, and then she gave me that high voltage grin that always made me go weak in the knees.

She said, "Would you like to join us?"

Walk, don't run, I told myself but couldn't help break into a jog as I headed to the bed.

They moved apart. I fell down in between them. They began to work on me, both taking turns giving me kisses, and then sharing one. I just laid there and thought about how pleased I was. I might not be rich or too successful but I was definitely the luckiest man in the whole world.

And the happiest.

Why we got married.

Carrie and I met at a bank in New York. She was from France exchanging money and I was just there getting a check cashed. We had both moved to NYC for our jobs. The insurance company I worked for had transferred me and she had a position in the ballet.

She didn't give me a second glance as we waited in line.

The first time I laid eyes on her, my legs almost buckled. She was breathtakingly beautiful. You've seen her in those dark French films smoking a cigarette and looking cool without even trying. She was *that* kind of French girl. She had long, natural blond hair. Beautiful, flawless skin. Big blue eyes with thick lashes that bumped into the glasses she sometimes wore. And her body? She was a ballerina, if that tells you anything. A ballerina with a set of tits which were *just* right. Not too big. Not too small. They sat up high and pointed at me whenever they were glad to see me. Just *perfect*.

It all seems very romantic and squishy, but it wasn't. I accidentally stepped on her foot and she let loose with a stream of French cursing. I left the building with my head down.

I saw her on the street a few weeks later. We locked eyes for one moment and I nearly tripped over my own two feet. I guess that's when I first felt love for her. Too bad she completely ignored me. And seemed to hate my guts.

Not that I'm some bumbling guy like you see in movies and on television. I don't "accidentally" get my foot stuck in buckets or find myself trapped beneath heavy objects. I was just klutzy around her. I mean, I'm hip. I look good, I know that. I have broad shoulders and big arms. I'm tall and I'm dark and I like to think I'm handsome without sounding like some sort of asshole. Chicks have always dug me. But even as great as I am, I knew that Carrie was way out of my league.

As I've said, the story—in the beginning—lends itself to the romantic sort. Two wayward souls seeking their fortunes in the big city. One a beautiful French woman and the other an ordinary Joe. Very romantic but highly unlikely.

But it did happen. And here's how.

One night I was getting hammered with some of the guys I worked with in a bar. I glanced at the clock on the wall around one in the morning and then at the door.

Carrie walked through it.

I felt myself go all jelly. It was like we were meant to be together. I was thinking, *There she was again!* How could it be possible with all the millions of people living in this city that she and I would cross paths more than once? *This was destiny! Destiny!*

I might also want to mention that I was drunk off my ass at the time.

But there she was. I couldn't stand to look at her because she was so beautiful, yet I couldn't look away. I really wanted to talk to her but I knew it would come out all wrong. And I kinda figured she hated my guts for stepping on her foot.

She sat at the bar. *By herself.* But instead of hearing warning bells, I heard violins. I really wanted to run away but I convinced myself I should give it a shot. What did I have to lose? Dignity? Self respect? None of that mattered. I was too drunk and too enamored to let it matter much.

I got up and approached her, trying desperately to act cool, which was the exact opposite of what I was doing. I was so nervous I was almost shaking. I sat down at the bar next to her and ordered another beer. She ignored me. I got up the courage once to say something but the look on her face—a cross between sadness and anger—keep my mouth shut. I looked away and told myself to leave. But then again, maybe *she* would say something—anything—to break the ice. She didn't. Apparently, she didn't even know I was there.

A little later, she picked up her cigarettes, downed the rest of her red wine and gave me a scornful look. I was toast and I knew it. But then she did a funny thing. She started off but not before saying, "Coming?"

Coming? Did that mean…? She just said that, didn't she? *Coming?* I glanced over at the guys from work and one of them gave a thumb's up and jerked his head towards the door, which she was disappearing through.

I jumped up and chased after her. We got into a cab. Not a word was said. I was suddenly very sober. As soon as the cab pulled away from the curb, she grabbed me and kissed me. I just sat there in shock. But soon I was kissing her back and when we pulled up to my building, we got out kissing. We kissed all the way to my apartment and there we fell on the couch and fucked. And I mean fucked. This woman fucked my brains out. She was insatiable. It was as if she had been celibate for years and I was her first man back or something. I was more than happy to oblige.

In the morning, I woke up to find her gone. Unfortunately, the story doesn't end there, as it should have.

Carrie showed up on my doorstep two months later. "I'm pregnant and it is yours."

· · ·

After we were married, she miscarried and has hated me ever since.

I don't like to say that, but it's true. She had to quit the ballet to marry me. She gave up a lot that she had worked years to achieve. She had been *this* close to becoming a prima ballerina. She was only twenty-six then. In a few more years, she would have been world famous.

Really. She would have been. She's a great dancer. I don't know shit about ballet and I absolutely hate it, but when she's onstage, good God! She's just great. But she had to give it all up because of me and my "sperm".

"You and your sperm," she would say from time to time. "Ah! What I lost because of it!"

And it was all for nothing.

I didn't mean to do it, for God's sake! I wasn't ready to settle down and get married either. Even to her. I had just moved to New York and wanted to play around a little until I found the perfect woman. But the perfect woman found me so it happened a little earlier than it should have.

She can be such a bitch. But because she's so gorgeous, she can get away with it and I let her. Any other man would, too.

I don't even know why we're still together, to be quite honest. I do love her, but we're just two very different people. She's French and you know how the French are. And I'm an American and French people hate Americans. But then again, don't the French hate everything that's not French? So, there you go. We didn't really have a good foundation to start with.

I asked her once why she stayed with me and she said, "You're funny. You make me laugh."

I eyed her. "You never get my jokes."

"No," she purred. "You are not a joke man. You do funny stuff."

I didn't know what the hell she was talking about.

"Besides, baby," she said. "No one gets your jokes. They're not funny."

See what I mean?

But she's great in bed and that woman can cook. Not to sound sexist, but she can cook very, very well. And she likes to do it. Believe me she doesn't do very many things she doesn't want to do. It's usually her way or the highway. So it's her way.

We lived in New York for a couple of years and then I got transferred again and this time it was down South, to Atlanta. She got a job at a dance school and began to teach ballet to little girls. We bought a nice house in the suburbs and lived a good life.

After we moved to Atlanta, I told her we could try for another baby if she liked.

She scoffed, "You are out of your mind! I teach those little bitches everyday! I won't come home to one!"

"Carrie, they're only, like, five years old."

She just stared at me. So that was that. She quit teaching ballet shortly thereafter.

Veronica.

Then she met Veronica.

Veronica was from some small town in Tennessee and had just moved to Atlanta. She was in her early thirties and set for life. Her super rich husband has just passed away.

"But, hell, he was almost eighty-six," she said and lit a cigarette. "He wasn't going to last that much longer. Thank God."

She and Carrie glanced at each other and squealed with laughter. I was a little taken aback but didn't say anything.

"Listen, honey," she told me. "I'm trailer trash and I married that old man for his money and you know what? He didn't give a shit so why should anyone else?"

"Oh," I said. "That's...cool."

"It is, isn't it?" she said with a smile.

I stared at her and shrugged. She stared back and gave me a slight wink like she had something on me. The way she looked at me made me very uncomfortable. But at the same time, it also made me curious. What was up with this chick? However, she didn't divulge any information. That's what made me suspicious of her. What I knew would fit into a thimble: She was incredibly beautiful—the brunette equivalent to Carrie—and she was incredibly rich. She drove this fabulous Jaguar that made my mouth water. She didn't seem pretentious and didn't pretend to be anything that she wasn't. Other than that, I didn't know shit.

She was still staring at me. I realized I had been staring at her. But when you've got a body like she did, what was a man supposed to do? It was as if her body was a feast. Where to look first? Her ass? Her legs? Her face? Eyes? Feet? Tits? I wanted to take it all in and at once, but I didn't want to overlook anything either.

I looked down at my plate. I was slightly ashamed of my feelings. Carrie was so great and so beautiful and here I was acting like a jerk. But damn! She looked good. Besides, all I was doing was staring. What was the big deal? I looked at her and smiled. She smiled back. Damn, she was hot.

But she was Carrie's friend and I was actually very happy that Carrie, after nearly four years in Atlanta, had finally made a friend.

They had met at Good Gourmet where Carrie sometimes shopped. It was a very expensive grocery store that has all kinds of international foods. She saw Carrie and smiled at her. Carrie smiled back. This was the first thing that piqued my interest about the two of them. Carrie never smiled at strangers. She rarely even smiled at me.

"She seemed so very nice," Carrie said happily.

"We started talking," Veronica said. "It was as if we had known each other forever."

Carrie smiled at her and said, "She is like the sister I never had."

Really?

Veronica eyed her for a moment before saying, "Anyway, she told me she taught ballet. Well, I just love ballet and have always wanted to study."

I just stared at her.

"I mean," she continued. "I don't want to be a ballerina, I would just like to study, you know, for the exercise."

"She's a very good student, too," Carrie told me.

"So she hooked me up and invited me to dinner, Clark," Veronica said. "May I have some more wine?"

This about brings us up to date.

I poured her some more wine and she and Carrie began to talk amongst themselves. I was so tired from the work day I didn't even really listen to what they were saying. Shopping, ballet, waxing. *Waxing?* I stared at them.

"I had that done once," Veronica said. "And never again."

"In France, everyone waxes there."

"Well, that may be true, Carrie," Veronica said. "But it just hurts too bad."

"Ice," Carrie said. "Numb it and you feel nothing."

Veronica considered. "I guess I could try that."

"It is the best way," Carrie said. "You will get used to it."

"If you say so."

They stared at each other and smiled. I stared at them. Carrie was never very friendly to anyone and here she was…she was being really nice to Veronica. It was weird. It made me happy that she was being nice but at the same time… *Why?*

"She is something else, oui, Clark?" Carrie said out of nowhere.

I shook myself. "What was that?"

Carrie was staring at Veronica who was staring back at her. If I didn't know any better…No. No way! There was just no way. Nuh uh. Nope. Forget it. Stuff like that only happened in porno movies.

Carrie smoothed the hair out of Veronica's face. She just sat there and let her do it, as if she enjoyed the touch of her hand.

I forced my eyes away from them. If they kept that up I would have to go to the bathroom and, uh… Do *that.*

Veronica turned to me. "Where are you from, Clark?"

Carrie answered for me, "Clark is from New York."

I cleared my throat and said, "Actually, I'm from Texas. Carrie always forgets that."

"We met in New York," Carrie said and smiled at her. "But his family is in Texas."

"Really?" Veronica said.

"I was transferred to New York with my job," I said. "And then they transferred me down here."

Veronica smiled. "Oh, cool."

Carrie said, "When I first saw him, I hated him on sight."

"Oh," Veronica said and grimaced a little.

"But then…" She turned and stared at me. "Something about this man I liked."

I couldn't help but smile at her.

"I can see it," Veronica said, surprising me.

"Oh?" I asked a little too high-pitched. I lowered my voice and said, "Really?"

She nodded and smiled slightly. "You're very…rugged. And you'd look good in a cowboy hat."

"I would?"

"Well, you said you were from Texas, Clark," she said. "And just let me say, not many men look good in cowboy hats."

Carrie turned to study me. "I see it."

I shrugged happily. "Well, if you say so."

Veronica looked at her watch. "Good grief, would you look at the time! I've got to go!"

She jumped up and grabbed her jacket off the back of her chair.

Carrie grabbed her hand. "Why not stay for a drink?"

"If I drink anymore I won't be able to drive home."

Carrie gave her a little smile. "Oh, you can stay longer, Veronica."

"No, really, I can't," she said. "I'd love to but I have an early appointment."

She glanced at me. I had been staring at her. I looked away quickly.

"But I will see you tomorrow for your lesson?" Carrie asked.

She nodded. "You bet!"

Carrie stood and they walked out of the dining room. I just sat there for a minute. Guess I should get up and tell her goodbye or something. They were at the door. Veronica was whispering something in Carrie's ear, but as soon as she saw me, she pulled away.

Well, that was a little odd.

"It was nice to meet you, Clark," she said as she opened the door.

"You too, Veronica," I said and gave her a wave.

She waved back and disappeared out the door. Carrie shut it behind her and turned to me.

"She seems nice," I said.

Carrie stared at me and her face lost all emotion. Her eyes narrowed. What had I done? Oh, God! What had I done? I knew I was in trouble. She always got that look on her face when I was in trouble.

She started towards me quickly. I took a step back. She backed me against the wall and pressed her lips against mine.

Oh, so that's what she wanted.

She began to gnaw at my face with her teeth, not really nibbling but gnawing, eating at me.

"I want you," she said and got down on her knees in front of me. "I want you now!"

I didn't have a problem with that.

She pulled my pants down and began to suck my cock. I just stood there and let her. She was very good at it. I ran my hand through her hair and she kissed her way back up my body, rubbing herself against my chest as she did so. I grabbed her by the shoulders and pulled her up and pressed my mouth against hers. Her mouth opened and her tongue flickered inside my mouth before I began to suck on it.

I walked her backwards over to the sofa and pushed her over the arm. Her ass was up in the air. I stroked it a little and lifted her skirt and pushed it up over her hips.

She didn't have any panties on!

I liked that. I bent down and kissed her ass, literally, running my tongue along her smooth skin. I loved her skin. It was so soft and nice.

"Fuck me," she begged.

I rubbed my cock along her ass, pushed her legs open and stuck it in. She gasped and began to push back against me. Soon we were fucking like crazy and she was panting. I was panting. She was wearing me out. I couldn't stop. She grabbed my hand and put it on her clit and rubbed against it until she began to come and when she came, she let out this animal like cry that sounded like, "Ekkkwwweeeekkkkkkk!"

That really turned me on. So much that I came on the spot and I came hard, imagining her and Veronica kissing each other.

After I was done, I hugged her middle and sighed with satisfaction. Now *that* was a good fuck. We stayed like that until she pushed me off, pulled her skirt down and said, "Please take out the garbage. It is getting stinky."

My friend Arthur.

So I was in a really good mood the next morning.

As I whistled on my way into the office, I got a few annoyed looks from the other people. These people were just a too little uptight. They were all very grim and seemed to hate their jobs, their lives and everything else they could think of to hate.

I kept to myself mostly. Except for Arthur.

I don't really even consider Arthur to be a friend. We just kinda got stuck with each other. We were both the new guys at the same time and had to go through all the orientation crap together. I would see him and say "Yo!" and he would see me and say, "What's up, buddy?"

I rarely invited him over to my house and I didn't even know where he lived. Arthur's a loser in an expensive suit. Not that I'm trying to be an asshole or anything, but he's pretty much worthless. He only got the job because his uncle's the vice president. I don't think he ever worked. Of course, he didn't have to. If anyone said anything to him, he went to his uncle who ironed it out. Besides, most people just didn't care what he did or when he did it. I know I didn't.

He was in my office by nine and, in his usual paranoid way, looked over his shoulder and around the office before he said, "So, it's like this, I met this chick last night and we clicked."

I glanced at him. He was making himself comfortable in the chair in front of my desk. I went back to the claim I was working on as he talked. He always tells me this shit, like I care.

"And then I get her home and she's got fucking nipple rings. In both tits! Nipple rings! All I can think about is the pain her poor breasts must have felt, which made me think about my mother, giving birth to me and enduring such pain."

He was so full of shit.

He added, "I couldn't get it up."

"Oh?" I said and glanced at him.

He shrugged and lit a cigarette. I waved at him to put it out.

"What is it?" he asked. "You smoke in here all the time."

"I know that," I said. "But I got a warning last week and if I get caught again, I'm in some serious trouble."

He eyed me but didn't put the cigarette out. "You get lot of girls with that accent, don't you, Clark?"

"My accent?"

"Yeah," he said and took a drag. "That good old boy Texas accent."

Good old boy accent. Odd as it may seem, it was harder to find a person in Atlanta with a Southern accent than a virgin in a whorehouse. Most people I met seemed to move into Atlanta from somewhere else.

I eyed him. "I'm married, Arthur."

"Still have to beat them off though, don't you?"

"I don't know what you mean," I said and went back to work. But, yeah, sometimes I did. The chicks liked me. What could I do? Unfortunately, I couldn't do a damn thing.

"Yeah, you do," he said dryly. "I'm a failure, Clark."

"Regressive therapy again?" I asked and glanced at him.

He nodded. "My therapist is insisting on it."

"That's nice," I said, then remembered the theater tickets he had asked to pick up for him. I took them out and handed them to him. "Here."

He stared at them, then back at me. "Are we going on a date, Clark?"

"No, you idiot," I said. "You wanted me to pick those up for you. Remember? For your mother?"

He stared at the tickets. "Oh, shit. I forgot. She doesn't want to go anymore."

"What are you going to do with them?"

"I guess I could scalp them," he said. "And I got four! One for her, one for me and one for my crazy aunt and her crazy friend. And now they don't want to go."

"Why not?"

"Someone told my mom it had some cussing in it."

"Oh," I muttered and studied the claim.

"What a waste of money," he said and shook his head.

"Too bad."

He took a drag off his cigarette, then ashed on the floor. "You want them?"

I shook my head.

"Come on," he said. "It's supposed to be a good play."

"I hate plays."

He eyed the tickets and mumbled, "*Gravy and Biscuits*. Now who in their right mind would name a play something like that?"

"Apparently the playwright."

"I don't even like gravy and biscuits."

"I do," I said. "In fact, I love gravy and biscuits."

"Why don't you take them?" he asked. "It's supposed to be a pretty good play."

"What's it about?" I asked.

"Southern stuff," he said. "That only old women would get a kick out of."

"I don't want them, Arthur," I said.

"Damn, what am I going to do with these things?" He waved them in the air just as the phone rang.

"Hello?" I said.

"Clark?"

It was Carrie. She never called me at work. Never. She didn't even want to know what I did all day. I once tried explaining it to her but she put her hands over her ears and said, "No! It hurts my head!" So why…? Oh. Must be because of last night. I could see why she'd call after that.

"Hey, baby," I said and smiled.

"Clark," she said. "Dinner with Veronica tonight. Somewhere nice."

"What does that mean?"

"Reservations," she said and sighed. "Could you make reservations?"

"Oh," I said. "I guess."

"Perfect," she said. "Somewhere very nice. I want to impress."

I thought about that. She wanted to impress. But why? Well, maybe because she had been friendless for so long and most people who met her didn't like her because of her French attitude. It was hard to make friends when you thought that everything in the world sucked except, of course, everything French. I could understand why she'd want to impress Veronica. However, we didn't really have the cash to impress.

"Why don't we cook?" I asked.

"I want to take her somewhere very nice, that's why."

"Baby," I said and lowered my voice. "You know that since we got the car worked on we don't have much cash."

Arthur eyed me. "Is that your wife?"

I nodded.

"That car is a piece of shit!" she snapped.

Like I didn't know that. It was an older model Audi and I don't even know why I bought it in the first place. Well, it had been cheap and I needed a cheap car. As soon as we could afford it, it was getting traded in.

Arthur said, "Tell her I said hi."

I ignored him.

"Clark, I am telling you," Carrie hissed. "Somewhere nice."

"Somewhere nice," I muttered.

Arthur waved the tickets and said, "Hey! Why don't we go together?"

I stared at him.

He grinned. "I can help you out, man!"

"Uh, listen," I said to Carrie. "Arthur here has a few tickets to the theater."

"I hate the theater," she said. "It is just people walking around and talking. Bullshit."

Well, she was right about that.

"Well, why don't we go?" I asked. "He has four tickets and Veronica can join us."

"Who's Veronica?" Arthur asked.

"Her friend," I told him. "How about it, Carrie?"

She sighed. "A nice meal afterward?"

"Sure," I said. "If the play doesn't get out too late."

"Is she pretty?" he asked.

I nodded and waved for him to shut the fuck up. "How about it, Carrie?"

"I suppose," she said. "Does Arthur have to come as well?"

"Yes."

"Merde!"

It should be noted that Carrie pretty much hated Arthur. He was oblivious to her feelings and thought she was just rude to everyone, which she was, only more so to him.

"So it's a date," I said.

"A date," she grumbled. "You tell him to be nice to Veronica or I will rip the son of a bitch's balls off his body!"

And with that, she hung up.

"So?" Arthur said.

"She'd love to go."

"Who is this Veronica chick?" he asked excitedly. "Is she hot?"

"Well—" I began.

"Is she hot? Girls with the name Veronica are either hot or look like grandmothers."

"Let's put it this way…" I said and put my feet up on the desk. "If I wasn't married, Arthur, I might consider fucking her. She's very *attractive.*"

"She's a dog. You're telling me she's a dog!"

Sometimes I could not figure this guy out. And I didn't really want to, either.

I asked, "What do you mean by that?"

"You said she was 'attractive'."

"Yes?"

"That's the word they use to describe *unattractive* chicks."

I studied him for a moment before shaking my head. "I consider Carrie to be attractive, so does that make her unattractive?"

"No! Of course not! Now if I had your sweet wife I'd never have to go to another singles bar again. I'd spend all my time fulfilling her desires."

Carrie would eat him alive. She really would. Then she would spit him out. In disgust.

"Well, okay, anyway, we'll go to the play and then if we have time, we'll go to dinner."

He nodded. "If she's a dog, I am going to be so pissed off at you."

"Arthur, this is not a date. We're going in a group."

He thought about that. "Oh."

I stared at him. He was very stocky. Well, that's a nice way of putting it. He was fat. And he knew it. I've told him to lose weight and he'd have an easier time getting girls, but he wouldn't listen. He also insisted on wearing a goatee, which did not suit him at fucking all. He wasn't a wrestler. Or a porn star. Or in a rock band.

"If you want to impress her," I said and touched my chin. "You might want to consider shaving."

He got up out of his seat and said, "Why? You going to kiss me?"

He thought he was so funny. He bent at the knees laughing. He could be such an ass.

"I was just thinking about that is all...I mean, I wasn't thinking about it, I was just...uh..." He stopped himself. "I gotta go."

He left and I went back to work.

After the snooze-inducing play, Carrie selected an Italian restaurant where the wait staff ignored us for the first ten minutes. It should be noted that Arthur was immediately smitten by Veronica, as most men were. And she disliked him on site. She whispered to me, "Who's the fat guy?"

It had been an interesting evening so far and I had a feeling it might get more interesting. If I could stay awake and enjoy it, that is. I was working way too many long hours and was about on the verge of nervous collapse. But I was working to get our bills paid off and then Carrie and I could go to France for a while. She told me that most people with foreign spouses make at least one trip a year to see their families. Since we'd been married, we'd only been once. I felt bad about it, so I worked over so we could go more often. That was the plan, though the plan might end up killing me.

Arthur tried to wave a waiter down and was ignored. He cursed under his breath and said, "I haven't eaten since lunch."

He grabbed a breadstick and began to gnaw on it.

Veronica eyed him and said, "We wouldn't want you to starve or anything."

Carrie giggled as Arthur's face took on a look of shock. I almost laughed too.

"What's that supposed to mean?" he asked her.

"She means you're…how do you say, Clark?" She snapped her fingers. "Well endowed."

If I had been drinking anything, I would have done a spit-take.

"Well, I'm certainly that," Arthur said proudly. "Right Clark?"

He realized what he said and looked away quickly. God, he got on my nerves so bad.

Veronica eyed him with disdain for a moment and said, "I'm just saying, Arthur, that if you stop eating so much, you'll lose weight."

"Do you think I need to?" he asked.

"Yeah," she said. "I do."

I almost cracked up.

A waitress appeared miraculously and asked if we had decided yet.

Veronica lit a cigarette and said, "No, not yet. But bring us a bottle of wine. Merlot."

The waitress nodded with approval and left.

Arthur whined, "Shit! What did you do that for? She'll never come back now!"

"Arthur?" Veronica said sweetly.

"Yes?" he said with a smile.

"Have you ever been on a *second* date?"

His smile disappeared.

"Here's a hint on how to score that second date, if you ever get it," she said sweetly. "Shut up!"

She went back to her menu, glanced over at Carrie and they smiled at each other. Carrie leaned over and whispered something in her ear and they both laughed.

Arthur watched them with a raised eyebrow. The waitress brought our bottle of wine and took our orders. Soon, we were all getting loaded and I was so tired from work I started dozing off.

Veronica was saying, "That happened to me so many times. He seems like a really nice guy but then he turns out to be a complete asshole. And then he won't leave me alone."

Arthur nodded like he knew what she was talking about.

She nodded once at him and turned to Carrie. "So, I was thinking we should go shopping tomorrow."

Carrie smiled almost as if…almost as if she'd been asked out on a date.

"But of course," Carrie said.

They stared at each other as if they were entranced. It was almost unsettling. I studied them and noticed Arthur doing the same thing. He glanced at me and mouthed, "Wow."

I cleared my throat and said, "So, Veronica, how are your ballet lessons going?"

She seemed to jerk at my question. "Uh, okay, I guess."

"She's a very good student," Carrie said.

Again, they smiled at each other. If I didn't know any better, I would say they liked each other. I don't mean liked, I mean *liked.* I don't know if I liked that. I mean, I liked the idea of it, but in reality, it was almost unsettling. What if Carrie liked her better than me?

Veronica said, "Oh, look at the time! I need to get going."

Carrie stared at her.

"Can I drop you, Carrie?" she asked as she put on her jacket.

What the hell...?

Carrie grinned. "Oui!"

"Uh, uh—" I began.

Carrie kissed my cheek and said, "I will see you at home."

They hurried off. Arthur stared after them and then back at me. I shrugged.

"Those girls really like each other, don't they?" he asked.

Maybe a little too much. Where the hell were they going? And what were they going to do?

Carrie didn't come home until very late. I had just fallen asleep in a chair in the living room when she slammed the front door.

I jumped up. "What is it?"

"Clark?" She eyed me. "Are you okay?"

I nodded. "I was having a weird dream... I...uh..."

I stopped talking and studied her. She looked a bit...disheveled. A little flushed. She looked like...she looked like... She'd been fucking! She had been out all night having hot sex! I could just tell. I could also smell it a little. She definitely had that sex smell about her. Before it could turn me on, it made me suspicious. Were she and Veronica going out picking up men and having sex with them? Was *that* the plan? I knew it! I knew Veronica wasn't anything but trouble. You can just tell with some girls. I could tell with her.

"Where were you?" I said and crossed my arms.

She walked past me and said, "Veronica wanted to show me her apartment. It's very nice."

She said "apartment" like "appartement". It was so sexy when she did stuff like that. Her French accent was so strong. I really liked it. But she looked like the cat that just ate the canary. She looked a little smug and a little flushed and...pretty damned sexy. But she was cheating on me!

If she thought she could fool me... Well, she couldn't.

"Oh, really?" I asked.

"Really," she said and took off her jacket.

"Really."

She grinned at me and sat down in my lap, putting her arms around my neck. She pulled me close to her and I breathed her smell in. I sniffed again. Perfume.

She was covered in perfume. That was the smell. Ummm…it was nice.

She gave me a kiss, running her tongue over my lips as she did so. Oh, like that was going to work. I started to pull away so I could interrogate her a little, but she pulled me to her and began to kiss me. Sure! Like I would just forget all about… Ummm…she was such a good kisser; she liked to nibble on the lips and…

I threw her down on the floor and fucked her brains out.

Dick for a day.

The next day, I had to attend a conference for work. It was boring, so I decided to ditch and go home early. I mean, why not? If my supervisor asked me anything about it, I knew enough to fake it. Besides, I had been working so hard I needed a break. I was going to spend the afternoon napping.

When I got there, Veronica's car was in the driveway. Fuck! How much time could those two spend together? I shook my head and parked behind Carrie's old MG Midget and got out. As I let myself into the house, I noticed it was really quiet. They were nowhere to be seen. I started to call out to Carrie, but then decided not to. I listened.

I heard voices coming from the bedroom.

I walked towards them. I heard Veronica say, "Oh! It's a very scary situation."

Ummm...

Carrie said, "But so fun!"

"I suppose," Veronica said. "I know this is weird, Carrie, but it's like I've known you my whole life."

I could tell they were smiling at each other.

"Me, too," Carrie replied quietly. "What were we talking about? Oh! Have you ever with...?"

"Oh, no!" Veronica replied. "Have you?"

What the hell were they talking about?

Carrie said, "It has been a long time for me."

"I've never done it," Veronica said.

"If you don't want to try…"

What the hell were they talking about?!

"Oh, no, I want to, it's not that! It's just… What if I do it wrong?"

Carrie said, "You let nature take over and nothing is wrong."

Nature?!

"Just like last night?" Veronica asked.

"Yes," Carrie murmured. "But we won't be so drunk."

I KNEW IT!

Veronica giggled. "Okay, then."

Carrie said, "I show you. We do this all the time in Paris. Like this."

I listened. I was more than sure she kissed her! I heard a moan and a

giggle.

"Like that?" Veronica said huskily.

"Oui," Carrie replied. "Now you try."

And then, oh, my God, I heard the unmistakable sounds of Carrie's vibrator starting. They were using a vibrator on each other!

I was beside myself! I was absolutely beside myself! But what could I do? Could I go in there? What would I say when they stopped what they were doing and looked up at me? *Oh, sorry, didn't mean to interrupt.* No. That wouldn't work. How about…*Carrie? Have you seen my green socks?* Then I would "notice"

Veronica and say, *Oh, hi, Veronica. Long time no see. What are you girls up to?*

Shit! I could never come up with any good lines. I should just give it up. But then... I pressed my ear to the door and heard the unmistakable sounds of a zipper being pulled.

They were beginning to get undressed.

Oh, good God. I wish I could go in there. I wished I had the balls to just throw open the door and let whatever happen, happen. I could; I could do it. But I couldn't. I couldn't because I didn't want to interrupt. I was actually pleased that my suspicious were confirmed but on the other hand... *Were my suspicions confirmed?*

Oh, God. My wife was having sex with another woman! It was a little mind boggling.

But what if she wasn't? What if she *was* and didn't want me to know about it?

I stepped back and thought about it. If they had wanted me to join in, they would have invited me. But then again, they both thought I was at work because, well, I was *supposed* to be at work. Was this their plan? To have an affair and never let me in on it? Now that wasn't fair, was it?

What *could* I do?

If I went in there, they would know I knew what was going on. And they might get mad. *You prick! You're so sneaky and vile and perverted! Get out of my face!* I could just hear Carrie say that. And then I wouldn't have a chance in hell of... What did I want? I wanted to be in there! I wanted to be in there fucking

and sucking and kissing and licking and panting and...
I wanted to be their dick for a day.

God that would be so nice!

First of all, I had to confirm my suspicions. I really, really, really wanted to make sure they *were* having sex and not just baking a cake or something. I had seen so many movies where they set it up like the women are having sex. We hear the sounds and the giggling. The guy gets all excited and nervous. He can't believe his luck! When he finally gets his courage up and goes into the room, the chicks are always just sitting around combing each other's hair or something. And he got all worked up over nothing. They never do anything like this in the movies. It's always a joke. And not a very funny one at that. Everyone in the audience always seems let down when it happens like that. And it always happens like that.

But they were doing it in my bedroom. They couldn't fake this. No way! Carrie and Veronica were having sex on my bed. Oh *GOD!* I could hardly contain my excitement. They were doing in my bedroom, on my bed. An image of them kissing each other came at me so strong I had to bite my fist for a moment.

I took a breath and came up with a game plan. It would have to be like I never heard/witnessed/fantasized anything. They couldn't know I was on to them. I would have to leave the house. I would call home like I was just *then* on my way in. I would tell Carrie I was coming home early and then see what happened. This would build trust and they wouldn't get "caught". If I "caught" them doing what I prayed they were doing, this might lead to embarrassment and knock me out of my chance to join in. I didn't want Carrie to think I was trespassing on her territory. I didn't want Veronica to think I was some sort of pervert.

These things have to progress naturally. I couldn't burst in there and flop down between them. I would have to be invited. I had to maintain some self control or I might not ever be invited into that bedroom. I couldn't interrupt. I had to leave and allow them their space.

I didn't want to leave.

Just a peek. I bent down and peered through the keyhole. I couldn't see shit! But I *could* hear them and if they were baking a cake, they were having one helluva good time doing it.

"Oh God oh God oh GOD!" Veronica cried. "Don't stop!"

I had to get the hell out of there. Otherwise, I wouldn't have been responsible for my behavior. So I got the hell out.

I drove around the neighborhood and decided to pick up a pizza. That would be so nice of me. I called the house to tell Carrie but the answering machine picked up. I guess they were still busy. The thought of them still being "busy" sent tingles up my spine. I shivered in delight.

I left a message, "Yes, darling, this is Clark. I'm off work now and will be picking up a pizza and bringing it home. Goodbye."

What a stupid message. Boy, she'll just jump and up and down with excitement, wouldn't she? *A pizza! How thoughtful of you! Now you can join Veronica and me in the bedroom!*

I growled to myself. A pizza wouldn't get me into that bedroom. What if I never got in? I stopped and thought about that. They just might be into each other with no plans to let me join in. They might just be having a secret affair or something. Well, that wasn't fair! Bitches!

But at least they weren't going around having sex with other men. No, those two were only interested in one another. That much I could ascertain from the noises coming from the bedroom. It made me feel a lot better and greatly increased my chances of being *the man* when they wanted *a* man.

But what if they never wanted one? What if? No. Fuck that. Every woman wanted a man, right? I thought about that. Oh, damn.

With pizza box in hand, I called from the front door, "I'm home!"

That was so unlike me. I never did anything like that. I was almost embarrassed.

Nevertheless, no one came running. I stomped into the kitchen and stopped abruptly when I saw Carrie at the stove stirring something in a pot and Veronica at the table flipping through a magazine. They were both dressed in little tank tops and panties. They looked like a couple of sorority chicks after a night of...doing what they had just done.

"Hello!" I called from the doorway.

They glanced up at me, then at the pizza.

"Pizza!" Veronica squealed and jumped up and ripped it out of my hands.

"Very nice, darling," Carrie said and walked over to the table where she and Veronica tore into the pizza like a pack of wild dogs.

"Hungry?" I asked and smiled at them.

With full mouths, they nodded eagerly.

I smiled again. "I'll just get a plate."

I walked over to the cupboard and took out three plates. As I turned back around, I was greeted by the site of two lovely asses hunched over the table. They were sticking right out at me. It took every ounce of self control I had to not run my hands over those asses. And I wouldn't have minded giving each a little slap, either. Just one. Carrie liked for me to slap her ass, and I liked to do it, especially when we were fucking. What did Veronica like? Would she like something like that?

"We were so hungry," Veronica told me and took a plate. "For some reason, I never thought about ordering a pizza."

Carrie nodded as she chewed. "I was going to prepare soup. That's all we had. I must go shopping."

Veronica turned to me. "Why are you home so early?"

"Yes, Clark, why?" Carrie asked.

I stared at her. She didn't say it suspiciously or anything, more with curiosity, as if I never did anything like this and she wanted to know why I had decided to start now.

I swallowed hard and asked, "Didn't you get my message?"

They shook their heads.

"Oh," I said and decided to lie, "The conference was cancelled."

"I just thought you would be late as usual," Carrie said.

I tried not to groan. Then I noticed something sparkly on Carrie's neck. I leaned in and looked closer. My eyes nearly popped out of my head. On her neck was a big fucking diamond necklace. It was so big and gaudy it didn't look real, which meant, of course, it was. What…when…where… It suddenly dawned on me. Damn. How the hell could I compete with that?

Carrie caught me staring and shook her head at me.

I pointed to her necklace. "What's that?"

"Oh, isn't it pretty? Veronica gave it to me," she said and played with it. "Like it?"

Like it? That fucker was worth more than our house!

"It's very nice," I said and stared Veronica dead in the eye. I knew her game! Trying to buy my wife's love with big diamond necklaces! Right! Like that would work!

Veronica looked away.

Carrie said, "The pizza is very good, Clark."

Let's see. On one hand we have pizza which is, in and of itself a very nice and delicious treat. On the other hand we have a very big diamond, which is...a very big diamond. Which would *you* chose? But what if... What if they only liked *each* other? The thought suddenly occurred to me. Could women do that? I mean, I knew they could, but could they do that, even if one of them was married?

I was screwed. I was so screwed. My chances of being dick for a day were gone. It was all about them, wasn't it? I knew it was. They didn't want me. They only wanted each other.

"Yeah, thanks for the pizza, Clark," Veronica said.

Like the pizza was that big a deal. Uh huh. Well, if that's the way it was going to be, so be it. Nothing I could do. I couldn't compete with Veronica and her money. I couldn't do shit. But they would at least tell me what was going on. I deserved that much.

"You're welcome," I said. "So what have you two girls been...*up to*?"

"We're going to the ballet," Veronica said.

"*Swan Lake*," Carrie said and smiled at her. "She has never seen it."

They were going to the ballet?

"Tonight?" I asked.

"Yes, tonight," Carrie said and smiled at me.

But they just went out last night. What if they weren't *really* going to the ballet and were going out to have sex with other guys? The kind of sex *I* wanted to have. Damn them. They were going out to find men! And they were going to have hot sex with them! I knew it! And here I was, a man, sitting right in front of them! I was going to waste!

No, wait. I'd already been through that thought process. It was the wrong one. They weren't seeing other guys. They were *seeing* each other.

"I could go with you," I said hopefully.

"You hate the ballet," Carrie said.

"That's not true," I said hurriedly.

She shook her head at me and turned to Veronica. "We must hurry if we are going to make our appointment."

"What appointment?" I asked.

"We're getting our hair and nails done," Carrie said.

"My treat," Veronica said and smiled.

"And then you're going to the ballet?" I asked.

They nodded.

They couldn't fool me. Ballet? No one goes to the ballet, even Carrie and she had been a ballerina. So where were they going? I thought about it. Probably to the ballet.

Carrie stood. "We must get going."

Of course.

She leaned over and kissed my cheek. "We will be home late."

We?

Veronica leaned over and kissed my other cheek. "Thanks again, Clark."

Yeah, thanks for nothing.

Fling.

I stayed up half the night waiting for them and finally fell asleep on the couch. When they got home—together!—they went to bed without waking me. Yes, they did. The only reason I knew they were even home was because I had woken up about three in the morning and decided to go to bed. Once I got there, I noticed there wasn't room in there for me. Veronica and Carrie were sleeping soundly next to each other and taking up the majority of the bed.

Bitches.

The thought of them together was driving me crazy. It ran through my mind all morning and all afternoon. I couldn't get it out no matter how hard I tried. I was so sleepy and fed up with obsessing that I fell asleep on my desk.

My door suddenly slammed and Arthur yelled, "You're fired!"

I bolted up and looked around wildly. "What is it? What is it?"

"Just kidding," he said. "Man, give me a cigarette."

He didn't wait for me to give him one; he just took one out of my pack and lit up as he eyed me. I really wished he would leave me alone. He was always in here bugging the shit out of me. I was in no mood for him. I had my own problems to deal with.

"Late night?" he asked.

"You could say that." I rubbed my eyes.

"Anyway," he said. "That Veronica chick is hot! I've got to call her. You got her number?"

"Last time I saw her she was in my bed."

Arthur's eyes nearly popped out of his head.

"No, unfortunately, *not* like that," I said hurriedly. "I mean, not literally, I mean…"

Hell, I didn't even know what I meant. But I didn't want him, of all people, to think about my wife and her… Her what? What was Veronica to her? How was she classified? How did Carrie think of her? Did she think of her as her "lover" as she sometimes called me? She better not!

I shook my head. Damn thoughts!

"Was she nude?" Arthur asked.

She might have been if I could have seen under the covers. But she had been covered from head to toe and snuggled up next to Carrie, probably having a good dream. They didn't even move when I came into the room. They just laid there and looked so damned good. It was really unfair when you got right down to it.

I backtracked, "No, I don't mean exactly… Look, Arthur, I don't think she s really your type."

"I know I could lose some weight," he said, indignant. "But she could lose some of that attitude. What'd she say about me?"

"She didn't say anything to me," I said. "She really only talks to Carrie."

"Wow. Now that's a fantasy, Clark."

"I haven't got a fantasy!"

"Maybe not, but I've got one." He winked at me. "Come on, man, give me her number."

"Haven't got it."

"Bullshit."

I shook my head. Veronica was a fling. She and my wife were only having a fling. It was an experimental thing. It would wear off. I would just have to sit back and wait for it to be over. I would be there for Carrie when it was. I might not ever get to have sex with Veronica, but at least my wife could. I wouldn't stand in her way. I was actually glad for her if she wanted to have sex with a woman; she couldn't have picked a better looking one than Veronica.

Arthur looked at me expectantly.

I said, "I'm telling you Arthur, she isn't your type."

"Then whose type is she?"

"My wife's," I muttered to myself.

"What?" he asked.

"Nothing," I said.

He studied me for a long moment before shouting, "Shut up and give me her number!"

I shook my head. "I don't have it and I won't ever be able to get it."

He stared at me. "Then I'll get it myself."

"Suit yourself."

He picked up the phone and said, "What's your phone number?"

"Why?"

"I'm going to ask Carrie for it."

I shook my head and gave it to him. He dialed. Now this should be good.

After a minute, he hung up the phone.

"What is it?" I asked.

"No one home."

Well, that figured.

Sacré Français.

After a good night's sleep, I awoke refreshed. This helped clear my mind and I could think about the situation objectively.

It really wasn't that big a deal when you got right down to it. So what if Carrie was having sex with Veronica? She could be doing worse things, like fucking some guy with a mullet. Or just fucking some *guy*.

The next day, I decided to do something nice for Carrie. I was going to buy her a gift. I hadn't bought her anything in a while and she deserved it.

I didn't admit to myself that the real reason I was doing this was so she might let me watch or even play a little with her and her new lady friend.

No, I was doing it because I was a good husband and that's what good husband's do. I could buy her things just like Veronica could. My gifts would be smaller in scale, of course, but nice nonetheless. She would appreciate them as much, if not more, than she did gifts from Veronica. I *was* her husband after all. I wasn't just some fling.

So the next day, after I bought my favorite sandwich (ham on rye) from my favorite downtown deli, I headed on foot to a jewelry shop. It was about eight blocks away and I had to bust ass to get there and get back within my lunch hour.

As I hurried and ate my sandwich and pushed past people to get to my destination, I saw someone who looked a lot like Carrie. Of course, it couldn't have been Carrie because she never came down here. She hated the downtown area. "Too busy and crazy!" she scoffed when I asked her to meet me for lunch.

But then again…

I turned and it *was* Carrie! What the…? Was she coming to meet me for lunch? Before I could smile, I spotted Veronica. Great! That's why she was here. Veronica probably knew of some fabulous little shop where they could buy…

They were headed to a lingerie store.

It was too much. I felt my feet move to follow them. I didn't care that my wife was cheating on me with another woman; she was going to buy lingerie with her! Lingerie! Maybe they would model it for me. As I neared them, I noticed something odd. They were holding hands! For God's sake! Were they in love or something? Could they *be* in love?

I dropped my sandwich.

No! They weren't in love! It was a fling! And even if they were in love, Carrie loved me more. Sure she did. And she could play all she liked with Veronica and…

Fuck that. I wasn't going to waste precious thoughts on that crap right now. I had before me a fantasy in the making. And between sex and paranoia, I would always pick sex.

So, I pushed all suspicious thoughts from my mind and concentrated on Carrie and Veronica. God, they looked good enough to eat. They walked side by side, *this close* to one another, giggling and acting like…girls. Mmmm… I liked that. They were both dressed in hip-hugger jeans and nice, tight sweaters. Carrie's sweater was pink, which was the best color for her, as it made her look divine and gorgeous and approachable, even if she wasn't.

Veronica's sweater was red. It really set off her hair and skin, too. She looked hot in it but totally unapproachable. She was the type of girl that everyone wanted to talk to, but they were afraid to at the same time. She might be nice, but chances were, she wasn't. At least I knew she was a nice person. If I wanted to approach her, I could. But at the same time, I was glad no one else knew *they* could.

I followed them to the lingerie store. They went in and I watched from outside as they picked up black teddies and red panties and the like. Oh, good God. They went into one of the dressing rooms together!

I kept my eyes on that door. It seemed to stay shut for a very long time. A little while later, Carrie came out of the dressing room, ran to a rack, picked up a few pieces of exquisite lingerie and headed back to the dressing room where Veronica was waiting on her.

"I love lingerie," I mumbled to myself.

An old lady walked by as soon as the words came out of my mouth. She screwed her face up and glared at me.

I said, "Purely in an academic sense."

I don't know where the hell that came from. Even so, it didn't work. The old bag spat at me, "Pervert."

I shook my head and ignored her and she stomped off. *Good riddance.* I went back to the window. They were now paying for their purchases which meant they would be out on the street again soon.

So they wouldn't see me, I ran down the block and waited until they came out of the shop. As soon as they fell in step with the crowd, I fell in step behind them.

Carrie was saying, "That was a very good shop."

"I know," Veronica said. "Did you pick up the thong? The one you tried on?"

I had to bite my fist as the image of them trying on panties came to me. A paranoid thought of never seeing them in their skivvies came as well, but I kicked it out of my mind. This was fantasy and nothing was going to fuck with it.

"Oui," Carrie said, then leaned over and whispered something in her ear.

Veronica pulled back and looked at her ass and gave it a little slap. Right there on the street! Right there! A few men stared after them. I glared at the men and kept walking.

They stopped at a hot dog cart. Veronica pointed to one in the pan. The vender pointed. She shook her head.

"Not that one, *that* one!" she told him.

"They're all the same," he muttered.

"Oh, that's where you're wrong," she said and gave him a knowing look.

The man stared at her, almost smiled then shook his head and got her *that* one. She took it and held it to Carrie's mouth.

"Want a bite, honey?" she asked.

Honey?

Carrie nodded and took a bite, chewed and said, "Umm, I like that."

The vendor asked Carrie, "And for you?"

"Just an ice cream," Carrie said.

He got her an ice cream cone. Carrie paid him and when he handed her the change back, she said, "Merci!"

Veronica stared at her and grinned. "I love that! Merci!"

Carrie grinned back and winked. "Merci!

Veronica ran her finger down the bridge of her nose and smiled back. "Merci!"

What the hell…?

They giggled and started off again. The vender stared after them, shook his head and let out a long, "Whheeeewww!"

They ate as they walked. Once Carrie held the ice cream to Veronica's mouth and when she took a big lick, some ice cream dribbled along her chin. Carrie leaned over, swiped it off with her finger and then licked her finger clean!

It was too much. I loved every second of it, but it was just too much.

They giggled, leaning against each other. I shook my head. Veronica slipped her hand into the back pocket of Carrie's jeans. Carrie put her arm around Veronica's shoulders and pulled her closer. They walked like that for a long time. Carrie once even gave her a peck on the cheek. Veronica reciprocated.

Most everyone on the street took a moment to stare at them and with good reason. Here were two drop dead gorgeous women feeling each other up in public! Most guys have to pay to see something like that.

But they didn't notice anyone else. They were in their own little world and no one could get in. Least of all me. And I deserved to be in! Carrie was my wife! I mean, *come on!* But all I could do was watch my wife stroll along the street with her...her...her...*her girlfriend!*

I was headed to divorce court. I just knew it. How could I not be? I was married to a closet lesbian. No wonder she was always so bitchy and rude, she wasn't living her life the way she wanted to! It made her tired and depressed and agitated. No wonder she hated me a good part of the time. She liked girls! There was nothing I could do and no way could I compete with that. No way. I shouldn't even put up a fight. I should just accept it and move on.

They got lost in the crowd. I couldn't find them after that and I was about sick and tired of it all, so I went back to work.

I decided against the jewelry and instead bought Carrie a huge bouquet of daises, which were her favorite flower. When I got home she was standing at the stove cooking. She didn't even glance at me when I entered.

"Hey!" I called and held out the flowers.

She eyed the flowers, smiled and took them. She pressed her face into the bouquet, breathed in and said, 'Merci. What did I do to deserve this?"

"Nothing," I said and really smiled at her. "You're just so beautiful."

She nodded in agreement and said, "We're having chicken with rice. Your favorite."

"Fantastic!" I said a little too enthusiastically.

"How was your day?"

She never asked me how my day was. *Never.* Guilt. She was feeling guilty! Didn't surprise me. It wouldn't hurt her to feel a little guilt. After all, she was having an affair with another woman! Actually, I didn't give a shit about her guilt. Or that she was having an affair. I just wanted her to share! That was my plan now. I had spent the entire afternoon thinking about it. Fuck all the paranoia. I just wanted one shot. One shot with her and Veronica. I would show them what I could do. All I needed was a chance. One chance, which I didn't have a chance in hell in getting.

"It was okay," I said, then casually, "Is Veronica here?"

"Oh, no," she said and threw the flowers on the counter disinterestedly.

No? She was always around now. And now she wasn't? Surely she and Carrie didn't break up already.

"She went to the store for soda," Carrie said.

Phew.

"She will be back soon, baby," she said.

Of course she would. She was hell bent on breaking up my marriage! She had to stick around to do that, didn't she? Well, I was going to tell her I knew her game. I knew what she was up to. She wanted my wife and I wasn't about to let her go without a fight. I was—

Stop paranoia! I had to stop it or I would go crazy. One minute I was fine with the affair and the next I was crazy. I couldn't win. But now I had my fucking game plan and I had to put it into action.

I stepped behind Carrie and put my arms around her waist. I nuzzled her neck and said, "You smell nice."

She stiffened and said, "What are you doing?"

"Just wanted to give you a hug."

She pushed me off and went to the sink and began to put dishes into the dishwasher. Maybe I was being a little too needy. But how else was I supposed to act? I was about to lose my wife! Sure, sure, I knew we weren't particularly compatible and all that other shit, but I just thought... I just thought if she left me, it would be for another man. The *other woman* aspect was making my mind go into a tailspin.

Fuck. I needed a Valium or something. My mind was going a mile a minute. I was thinking so much that I had a headache.

Just then Veronica walked in. "Hey Clark!"

"Hey," I mumbled and eyed her. I was almost beginning to dislike her. She was always so *nice.*

"Did you get the sodas?" Carrie asked.

She held up a twelve pack of beer. "Changed my mind."

Changed her mind... What did she mean by that? Did she mean...?

She turned to me and said, "It's imported. I thought you might like imported."

I studied the beer. It was Bass. Good beer.

"Nice," I said but didn't smile at her. What was *her* game plan? Did she have a game plan? And if she did, did she—

"You're being all grouchy," she said. "Is he always like this, Carrie?"

Carrie sighed, threw her hands up in the air and said, "Always!"

I jerked my head over towards her. *I* was the one who was always grouchy? Me? What world did she live in?

Veronica set the beer down on the table and said, "You're spoiling for a fight, aren't you?"

Okay. Stop right here. This woman was going to fight me now? This itty bitty woman? She was going to fight me? Why? Oh, yeah. I could see it. She was going to show Carrie how tough she could be. She wanted to be the "man", did she? I'd show her. I wasn't about to play that game. I knew if I hit her, she'd turn the whole thing around and tell Carrie I was abusive and that she should leave me. Yeah. Like I was going to fall into *that* trap. Right.

"No," I said and crossed my arms. "I'm really not."

"Well, I am," she said and grinned and punched me playfully. "Come on! Put 'em up!"

I just stared at her.

"Come on," she said. "It'll be fun!"

Oh, I'll tell you what would be fun. Me and you and my wife and... She hit me on the arm. It hurt.

Carrie laughed. "Clark, you should see your face!"

I ignored her and said, "Veronica, don't do this."

"Do what?" she asked and hit me again.

"Ow!" I said and rubbed it. "What the hell did you do that for?"

"Come on, Clark!" she squealed. "Let's duke it out!"

This girl was crazy. I liked that.

She kept at it until I put 'em up. I didn't have much fucking choice. We walked around each other and pretended to throw punches. She got a mischievous smile in her eye and took a full swing and punched me on the nose as hard as she could. I was knocked out cold. I fell on the floor with a thump.

Carrie screamed, "Merde!"

Every man's fantasy.
Realized.

I came to on the couch. The first thing I noticed was that my shoes were off. And the second was that Carrie was holding an ice pack to my nose, which throbbed with pain. And the third was that Veronica sat on my other side with a wet wash cloth, which she pressed to my forehead from time to time.

"Here he is!" Carrie squealed. "Oh, baby!"

She hugged my head to her chest. I couldn't breath. I fought against her until she released me.

"Are you okay, Clark?" Veronica asked "I swear, I didn't mean to hit you."

Sure she didn't.

"Are you okay?" she asked again.

"Just a little dizzy," I told her and tried to sit up.

She pushed me back. "Easy there. Is your nose broken?"

"You tell me."

She and Carrie sat back and stared at my nose. They glanced at each other and shrugged, then Carrie leaned in closer, so close I could feel her breath on my face. She smelled like wine and cigarettes.

"It's swollen," she said. "But not broken."

I felt it and winced. It hurt like a motherfucker.

"Here," Carrie said and pushed a glass of water in my face. "Drink."

I took a sip, and then pushed it away. I stared at them. They were being really nice, too nice if you ask me. And I was sick of it all. I mean, I wasn't going to get anywhere with these women. They knew what they were all about and kept me in the dark. And they also knew every move in the book to keep me hanging on like some dumbass. I was an amateur compared to them. I decided then and there to give it up. They could do what they wanted to do. I wasn't going to plead or grovel or do any of that other shit. And if they were in love and ran off together, so be it. I was so tired of speculating.

I sighed and stood. "I think I'll just go to bed now."

"Oh, no," Carrie said and jumped up. "We have to eat."

"Not really hungry." I started off but she grabbed my hand and Veronica grabbed my other hand and forced me to stop walking.

"Let's eat," Carrie said.

Okay, I guess I could eat a little something.

I allowed them to lead me into the dining room. They sat me down and pulled up chairs on either side of me. That was odd. I watched as they prepared a plate of food and put it in front of me. Veronica poured me a beer and held it to my lips.

"It's good," she said and nodded.

I shrugged and took a sip and Carrie pushed a fork at my mouth. I opened my mouth and she slid the fork in, staring at the food until I took it off the fork and began to chew. Once I did, she smiled at me and kissed my cheek.

"Good?" she asked and nuzzled my neck.

"Very," I replied.

Veronica got up and put on some music. Beatles. *The White Album.* My favorite. How did she know that? Did she know that? Had she—

I stopped myself. I wasn't going there ever again. What would be will be. And that's all it would ever be. So be it.

Yeah.

"Good chicken with rice, oui?" Carrie said and smiled.

I took another bite. It *was* good.

They continued to feed me, each taking turns. They wiped my mouth for me and then they…they began to feel me up.

I was probably imagining it.

But their hands lingered on my knee and then they moved towards my crotch. Just before the hands got there, they stopped and giggled.

No. This just wasn't happening. It was just a dream and I would wake up with a hard-on. I would jerk off, shower, shave and then go to work. I would work all day, come home and maybe watch some TV.

Their hands were now on my arms. Veronica said something about my arms being so big and strong. I had only heard stuff like that in my dreams and on stupid TV shows, so I ignored her.

"He is a very good man," Carrie said. "So strong and sweet and good and kind…"

Bullshit. She never talked about me like that. Her kind words didn't get my hopes up. I just sat there and let whatever happened happen. And nothing was going to happen. It was either a dream or some big tease. More than likely a tease.

"Oh, you got a little chicken on your chin," Veronica said and leaned over and licked it off.

"I see that," Carrie said and licked the same spot that she had.

"Mmm…" Veronica said. "You taste good."

"Oh?" I said and tried to remain cool. I *had* to be cool about this. Especially since I didn't think anything was going to happen. That way I didn't end up looking like a big jackass. They would probably laugh at me. *You thought we were going to do what?* I could hear them now. My ego would be crushed. I would have to smile sheepishly and pray they never brought it up again.

"So good," Veronica said and slid her tongue down my throat. "If I was a vampire, I'd eat you alive."

Really?

"So would I," Carrie said and began to nibble at my neck. "Oh, baby, you do smell delicious."

My dick was so hard it hurt.

Their hands were all over me. They were caressing my chest and my neck and my back and my face. They ran their hands through my hair and kissed my cheek and my forehead and my…

Oh, good God. They were getting down on their knees.

Wake up! I had to wake up! But it was real. It was really happening. Even if I didn't believe it and couldn't comprehend the enormity of it, it *was* happening.

Oh, my God. It was happening!

I stared down at them and Veronica unzipped my pants. She and Carrie helped each other pull them off as they stared up at me. I couldn't move. I couldn't think. I couldn't do anything. But I most definitely was not going to get up and leave the room.

And then I was naked from the waist down. My dick throbbed. They stared at it and Veronica smiled with what I hoped was approval. She leaned over and took the whole thing in her mouth. She deep-throated me for a moment and then came back up, then went back down again. Then she offered it to Carrie who did the same. They began to lick and nibble on my dick, suck on it until I thought I was going to explode. They kept at it until I did, until I came. I shot white cum across the room. It landed on the wall with a *thump!* Their eyes grew wide and they stared after it then back at me. They burst into laughter.

"Clark," Veronica said, laughing. "I've never seen anything like that before."

Neither had I. I didn't even know I was capable of shooting across the room like that. Well, I guess you learn something new everyday.

Carrie smiled and said, "Let's go into the bedroom."

They helped each other up, grabbed hands and started out of the room. They were still dressed. Both were wearing short skirts and little white tops. And high heels.

This couldn't really be happening. Nevertheless, I jumped up and ran after them. I found them settling on the bed. They didn't hesitate and started kissing each other immediately. They were on their knees, holding onto each other by their waists. They went right to it, sucking and running their tongues along each other's mouths and sucking face and...

Oh, wow. I was hard again just like *that.*

They began to undress hurriedly as if they couldn't get out of their clothes quickly enough. As soon as they were naked, they fell back on the bed and their legs intertwined with each other's and their wet pussies touched. They began to rub against each other, scissoring their legs together. They kissed and ate at each other's breasts as their crotches rubbed against each other's and the moans started.

Carrie glanced over at me and said, "You coming to bed?"

Veronica smiled at me. I was in. I was in! I was in! I was in in in in in! *YESSSSSS!*

I jumped on the bed and they pushed me down and started kissing me all over. They licked and probed and touched every square inch of my body and took turns giving me head. Each had a different technique. Carrie nibbled, deep-throated and licked. Veronica liked to suck and I mean suck. She sucked hard. It was wonderful.

They did this for a little while until they pulled back and at the same time, with haste, each of them tried to climb on top of me. They nearly pushed each other off the bed as they both tried to mount my throbbing cock. They stopped, laughed nervously and stared at each other.

"You go first," Carrie said to Veronica.

"Oh, no, you," Veronica said and smiled.

"No, you," Carrie said, smiling. "You go now."

"Sure?" Veronica asked and glanced at me.

I nodded quickly.

"Okay," Veronica said.

Oh, God. Here it was. I was going to fuck her! And Carrie was going to fuck me after I fucked her! And then I could fuck each of them again and then—

Veronica grinned and kissed me. She sucked on my tongue as Carrie kissed her breasts. I just laid there. She bit her bottom lip, rolled over onto her back and opened her legs.

I got between them.

I slid my cock into her tight (and it was oh, so tight) pussy and this wonderful feeling come over me. I had forgotten what a new woman felt like. She was totally new to me and that made it all the more exciting. What was more exciting was the fact that Carrie was now kissing her as I fucked her. Veronica pushed back at me as I fucked her and told me several times to do it, "Harder!"

I did my best. Sweat was dripping from my forehead. They were sweaty too. We were all so turned on and horny nothing could have stopped us from fucking.

As I was about to come, Veronica pushed me off her and she and Carrie grabbed my dick with their hands and finished me off, then they sucked me dry.

If I died at that very instant, I would have died a happy man.

As I waited to get hard again, they went at it. They moved all over that bed and grunted like animals in their lust. They kissed and licked and played with each other as if they couldn't get enough. I know I couldn't. I could have watched them all night. But then again, it's always more fun to play.

When I was hard again, Carrie climbed on top of me and rode me hard, grabbing onto the bedpost. Veronica kissed me as I fucked my wife and after I came that time, we took a shower together. They rubbed up against each other up and up against me. We ended up on the floor, me fucking Veronica doggie as she licked and ate Carrie's pussy.

We moved back to the bedroom. Veronica lay down on her stomach with her ass in the air and sucked my cock as Carrie ate her out from behind. She would pause from time to time, pull Carrie up and kiss her and then she would kiss me. I was just so turned on, I was in heaven.

This went on half the night. It was all hands and legs and asses and tits and pussies and in the middle of it all, one very hard cock. I was so proud of that, that it was *my* hard cock that was pleasing them to no end.

When I fell away exhausted again, they went at each other. I didn't ask any questions. I wasn't a fool. I just sat back and watched.

Carrie began to kiss Veronica's naked body. As she did so, she murmured to her in French. I made out some of the words, "delicious", "beautiful", and "sublime". They were others, many others, but my French wasn't that good.

I smiled because she sometimes did the same thing to me. It was different now because I could see how she looked when she did it to me. It really turned me on and before I knew what I was doing, I was between them again.

We were up late, so I slept through my alarm. When I finally awoke, they were sleeping peacefully next to me, curled in each other's arms. I stared at them, at these two beautiful women and I just had to pinch myself.

Yeah, it hurt. Which meant it had really happened.

Welcome to the exciting world of ménage.

Arthur said, "What are you looking so jolly about?"

"Am I looking jolly?" I asked and stared at the reflection of myself in the window. Yes, I suppose I was looking a *little* jolly. Nothing wrong with that. I mean, I had just had a ménage a trios, hadn't I? Yes, I had and with two beautiful and exciting women. I had a right to look jolly.

He sat down and said, "I can't get Veronica's number."

If I had anything to do with it, he never would.

"She's perfect for me," he lamented. "She's everything I could ever want. She's smart, sexy, pretty, beautiful, has a nice body and doesn't seem to be too disgusted with me."

I decided to set him straight, "Veronica is…how do I put this?"

"I know, I know," he said. "She's not my type."

He had that right.

"I just really like this chick," he said. "I bet she'd good in bed."

"She is," I said before I could help myself.

He turned to me, his mouth half open and said, "What?"

"Nothing," I back peddled. "I mean, she *looks* like she would be good in bed."

"Back up!" he said. "You agreed with me! Did you fuck her?"

I sighed. "Listen, Arthur, I'm going to set you straight. Carrie and Veronica and I have a very special relationship."

"What the hell does that mean?"

What *did* it mean?

"Are they..." he started and waved his hand. "...are they lesbos?"

"Not exactly."

"And...?"

I took a breath. "Carrie and Veronica *really* like each other and they *really* like me, too."

"You?" he spat. "Why would they like *you*?"

"Well, I don't know to be honest," I said. "I mean, I am Carrie's husband and Veronica is a close, personal friend of hers, so I guess it only makes sense that they would like me."

He stared at me.

I added, "But they do like me. Very much so."

"Let's cut the shit, Clark."

"Alright."

"Did you fuck Veronica?" he asked and narrowed his eyes.

"I did."

"Man! You suck ass!" he roared. "What does Carrie think of that?"

"She didn't mind," I said.

He nearly fell out of his chair. "She didn't mind?"

"No," I said, very proud that I could say it. "She was right there and didn't mind a bit."

He was so flabbergasted that he couldn't speak. He also looked a little deranged. Maybe I shouldn't have said anything. He didn't look like he was taking the news very well.

"So you had a threesome with them?" he asked, shaking his head.

"Yes," I said. "I did."

"*You* had a threesome with them?"

"I did."

"You're lying."

"I'm not," I said

"You did not have a threesome with them!"

I held up my hands. "Swear to God."

"You son of a bitch!" he roared. "Son of a bitch!"

"What can I say? I have a certain quality that attracts the opposite sex."

"You stole my girl!"

I rolled my eyes. "There was no stealing involved! Besides, they seduced me!"

"How am I ever gonna get a date with her now? Aw, man, you suck!"

"Come on."

He glared at me. "It's your looks. Women dig your looks."

"Nothing I can do about that."

"And your cowboy accent," he said, fuming.

"It has nothing to do with the way I talk. Nothing."

"You're probably right. I'm sure it has *nothing* to do with the way you talk. Can I help it if I was born here and didn't get a cute accent? Huh!" He shook his head and grumbled to himself, "You son of a bitch."

I knew then that I shouldn't have told him but I was dying to tell *someone*—anyone. It had happened to me and I was ecstatic! I never thought I would actually have a threesome though I had had fantasies about it ever since I was little kid. And I wanted to share. Or I wanted to brag. Same difference.

Arthur grumbled again, "You son of a bitch."

Ah, well. Jealousy can make a person bitter. Wasn't my problem he didn't get a threesome and I...*DID!*

When I got home, they were preparing dinner. Steak and potatoes. Another favorite. *What did I do to deserve this?* Because I was tha' man! That's why!

"Hello big man," Veronica said and then added, "And I do mean big."

I almost blushed.

"How is my baby?" Carrie asked and kissed my cheek.

"I'm a new man, thanks to you," I said and put my arms around her.

"And Veronica."

"Oh, let's not forget Veronica."

"Yes, let's not," she said and gave me a kiss. She put her arms around Carrie and we stood there and hugged until the timer went off on the oven.

"So, how was work?" Carrie asked as she put on a pair of oven mitts.

I loosened my tie and said, "Oh, it was such a hassle. I've never had such a fucking bad day! I tell you—"

Veronica interrupted, "Did you get the clothes out of the dryer, Carrie?"

"No! I forgot!"

"I'll get them," she said and headed out of the room.

"I'll go with you," Carrie said and followed her.

"Well," I said and sat down at the table. I turned and stared after them. Were they going somewhere? What were they doing? Oh, the clothes. Yeah. But what if—

No. I wasn't about to let that paranoid shit get to me again. Especially after last night. Nope. They were just going to the dryer and then they'd be back. But what if... Stop it.

I stopped it.

After we ate dinner, Carrie and Veronica folded clothes in the living room. I sat behind a newspaper and tried not to pay any attention to them.

They suddenly squealed with laughter. I looked over the paper and studied them with one raised eyebrow. They both had a pair of my boxer shorts on their heads. They looked cute. And so sexy. They were so funny. And—

I went back to the paper, shaking it and clearing my throat to let them know I was, in fact, in the room just in case they…they…needed me for anything.

Again, the giggle. This time less pronounced. I peered over to see Carrie holding onto Veronica's hand. They pressed their noses together. What were they? Eskimos?

Nevertheless, that was a good sign. Maybe we could get started soon. I was tired as fuck and didn't want to be up all night. But I could stay up if they wanted me to. They would just have to let me know.

But then…

Veronica stood and said, "I have to get going. Thanks for letting me stay for dinner, Clark."

I nodded. "You have to go so soon?"

"She has an early appointment," Carrie said.

She walked her to the door and I heard them quietly whispering for a moment before I heard it close. What if…? What if they were sneaking out together?

"Oh, Carrie?" I called.

"Yes?"

I went back to the paper and muttered, "Just checking."

Veronica didn't come by the house for about a week. I had pretty much decided that our one night of wild monkey sex was just a once in a lifetime thing. Maybe I had dreamed it. Whenever I asked Carrie about Veronica, she would just shrug and say, "She is a very busy person."

So I stopped asking. I didn't really want to pressure her. I mean piss her off.

Another thing. Arthur suddenly stopped coming into my office every hour on the hour. When I would see him in the hall, he'd ignore me. I tried several times to talk with him but he'd just push past me and head in the other direction.

I finally saw him in the restroom. I ignored him and took a piss on the far side of the urinals. He ignored me as well. Like I cared.

But I decided to be a nice guy. I mean, I was a nice guy and just because he was a jealous asshole didn't mean I had to stop being nice. I wasn't into that alpha male crap. It took too much work.

As we were both washing up, I asked him nicely, "How's it been going, Arthur?"

He eyed me and hissed, "What's it to you?"

I was a little taken aback. "Why do you have an attitude? You never come see me anymore."

Just then, this little weasely guy came in and went to the urinal. I cleared my throat and kept washing my hands.

Arthur cut the faucet off and said, "Well, for starters, you slept with my girl."

I rolled my eyes, cut my faucet off and shook my hands into the sink. I wasn't going to reply to that.

He shook his head and lit a cigarette. The little weasely guy came over and said, "You can't smoke in here, sir."

He took a deep drag then threw it in the sink. The weasel smirked at him and walked out without washing his hands.

Arthur lit another cigarette. "So, tell me, is she good in the sack?"

I stared after the weasel. "What do you mean?"

"Veronica. Is she good in the sack?"

I didn't see any reason to upset him more, so I said, "I really can't remember."

"Liar."

I groaned and said, "Yes! She was good!"

"So she was good?"

Fine, I'd give it to him straight, "Well, now that I think about it, she was good. Very good, in fact."

"You son of a bitch."

"Why all of the sudden the anger and hostility, Arthur?" I asked. "Are you that jealous?"

"Yes, I am!" he grunted. "I mean, why you? You're not that attractive."

"Apparently I'm attractive enough."

"Whatever," he said and threw his cigarette down. "You can go to hell."

And with that, he stomped out of the restroom.

As soon as I opened the front door that night, Carrie and Veronica pounced on me. Wow. She was back! And both of them seemed really happy to see me! But then I noticed that Arthur was sitting on my couch.

What the fuck?

He had a lot of nerve. Who did he think he was coming into my house and talking to my girls? I mean to Carrie and Veronica.

"Clark!" Carrie squealed. "You are home!"

Veronica said very enthusiastically, "Hi, Clark!"

Arthur gave me a curt wave.

"Hey, Arthur," I said and took off my jacket. "What are you doing?"

"I just dropped by to ask Veronica to dinner," he said and crossed his arms.

My eyes narrowed at him. This was the first time I had seen her in a week and he thought he was going to waltz in and take her to dinner? I didn't think so.

Veronica whispered in my ear, "He just came in and we couldn't get him to leave. We were thinking about calling the cops."

I nodded and stared at Arthur, who was making himself cozy on the couch. Carrie just glared at me and threw up her hands.

"Make him leave, Clark," Veronica whispered. "What does he want?"

I shrugged, but I knew. He wanted Veronica. He was so weird. Couldn't he take a hint? She didn't like him. He needed to move on.

"Clark," Carrie said without lowering her voice. "He must go. We have dinner reservations."

We do?

"Well, no," Veronica said and whispered again, "I'm cooking for y'all tonight. It was supposed to be a surprise until *he* showed up."

I nodded and walked over to Arthur. "So, Arthur, what do you want?"

His face flushed. "Nothing to do with you."

He was drunk. I could smell the liquor on him. I wondered how I could get rid of him without a struggle. I really didn't want to embarrass him. But then again, he didn't seem to mind embarrassing himself, so why should I?

I was just about to do something when Carrie stomped over to him.

"She doesn't want to go out with you," she hissed. "Now go."

Arthur just stared at her.

She went over and protectively put her arm around Veronica. They both gazed at him with contempt. If I was him, I would have been out the door. You don't ever want women to turn on you like that, especially when there are two of them.

"Really Arthur, you should go," I said.

He finally got the hint and his head dropped. I felt kind of bad for him. But, hell, what did he expect? You just don't barge into someone's house and start demanding things.

He stood up and walked towards the front door, then turned around. "Listen, you people can have each other. I've seen enough."

And he left.

"What the hell was that all about?" I asked.

They shrugged.

I stared after him wondering if he was, in fact, crazy. He could have been. I didn't know him that well. I'd have to keep my eye on him from now on.

"Anyway," Veronica said. "Are you ready?"

All thoughts of Arthur ran out of my mind. Was I ready? Oh, yeah, you could say I was. It had been an endless week of fantasizing about our next...Our next...*trios*.

I unzipped my pants and was about to take my shirt off when Veronica stopped me and said, "No silly! I mean are you ready to go?"

Oh, shit. I was such an asshole!

I pulled my pants back up and said, "Oh, right!"

She and Carrie cracked up. They pointed at me, bent at the knees and howled with laughter. Ha ha. It was kinda funny. They were nearly rolling in the floor. I wish they would stop.

Soon they did and she threw me the keys to her Jag. "You can drive."

Veronica had one of the nicest penthouses in the state of Georgia. Forget that. In the world. It had a huge sunken living room and a marble Jacuzzi and a gigantic kitchen. It looked like one of those swank bachelor pads from the sixties. It was modern and spacious and cool as shit.

"This is great!" I told her as I took it all in.

"It's just a rental," she said and smiled. "My lease is up next week."

"Too bad," I said and walked around. It was most definitely the nicest place I had ever been in. I wouldn't mind living here. I could imagine myself in a smoking jacket with a highball glass in one hand and both arms around Veronica and Carrie's shoulders sitting on the twelve foot velvet couch. We could have so much good sex here.

She nodded and smiled. "I'll go check on dinner. Clark you make yourself a drink and Miss Carrie, I would like some assistance in the kitchen."

Carrie squealed with delight and grabbed her hand. I watched as they disappeared out of the room.

After I prepared myself a scotch and water, I took a walk around the place. It was so nice. I knew I'd never own anything this nice, but it was good to be here all the same.

I went into the bedroom and my mouth dropped at the gigantic bed covered with a mink—yes a mink—comforter or duvet or whatever the fucking hell they're called. It looked nice. I imagined myself laying my two pretties right there on top of it and then snuggling afterwards.

I smiled to myself and stared at the closet door. Did I dare? I stopped and listened. They were still in the kitchen. Sure. Why not? I threw open the door and was greeted with a walk-in closet that looked like a fancy boutique. There were four or five racks of clothes and a whole wall of shelves filled with shoes.

I walked around a little and finished off my scotch. This was a lot of shit. She would never be able to wear it all. And I had never seen her in anything other than jeans and sweaters and the occasional t-shirt.

"My husband," I heard from behind me.

I whirled around. Veronica smiled at me and handed me another scotch and water.

"Thanks," I said and took it.

"My husband bought me all this stuff," she said and touched a mink coat.

I nodded and sipped the drink.

"I want to get rid of all of it but every time I start to throw it away, I get…" She held her hand over her heart. "…sick."

"I'm sorry," I said.

She nodded. "Henry was the best husband ever."

"Ever?"

"He was my second husband," she said and nodded.

"Second?"

"Yeah, so?"

"Oh, nothing." I took a sip of my scotch and asked her, "What happened to the first?"

"The first?" she asked and clucked her tongue as she glanced at the ceiling. "Ummm…he was an asshole."

"Oh?"

"Yeah," she said. "He was a bum who didn't know the meaning of the word *work*. He liked his bong and beer more than he liked me."

"You're joking."

She shook her head. "I was still married to him when I met Henry."

"That must have been messy."

"It was," she said and smiled. "He got what he deserved, though."

"How's that?"

"Oh, he…nevermind."

"No, go on," I said. I really wanted to know.

"It wasn't a big deal," she said and went to the bed. She sat down and patted the place beside her. "Come here."

I walked over and sat down. "So you divorced him?"

"Yup, and at the ripe old age of twenty-two."

"You were that young?"

She smiled at me. "Have I ever told you I just love your accent? I mean, I know I've got one too, but yours is so…*masculine.* Like a cowboy's."

Actually, she had told me she liked my accent. And Carrie had told me, too. It was a ladykiller thing to have, I do have to admit. Women just loved the whole Southern accent thing. The good old boy who was a stud in bed that would make you moan with delight but you could still take home to mama. Yeah. I had it. It was good thing to have.

I nodded and said, "So how long were you married to your second husband?"

"Ten years," she said. "We were together for ten years."

"Wow," I said. "Congratulations on that."

"It wasn't hard," she said. "He let me do about anything I wanted to do and he was…"

I finished for her, "…a little old."

She eyed me. "What does age have to do with it?"

"I don't know, I…" I couldn't think of a thing to say.

She leaned back on the bed and said, "I loved him, I really did. It might not have been a romantic love, but I did love him."

"Romantic love?"

"Romantic love," she said and sat back up. "You know you start out with that most times, but Henry and I didn't. We started out as companions, with companion love."

I nodded like I understood.

"Besides, romantic love wears off," she said. "Sometimes."

"Sometimes?"

She bit her lip and grinned. "Sometimes."

"Oh?"

She nodded. "He was very good to me and I miss him everyday. I really do. He was a good old man."

I nodded.

"It's just…" She stopped and looked away. "I mean, it's hard to find…friends. He was my friend."

I nodded. It was hard to find friends. No one ever tells you that when you're a little kid. You always think you'll be able to trust people and have lots of friends. But when you grow up and get married, people start disappearing from your life. And then it's hard to replace them because, well, most people have their own lives. It had been very hard on Carrie and me to make friends once we came to Atlanta. Sure, we went out with a few couples and had dinner, but we hadn't been able to make any lasting bonds. Of course, Carrie didn't like most people. Suddenly, I was so glad she and

Veronica had met. She had a friend now. I was so proud that she had met someone she could relate to.

"Clark," Veronica said and stared into my eyes. "Thank you for opening your home up to me. Thank you for being my friend."

I stared at her. Was that what we were? Friends who had really hot sex? Hell that was cool with me.

"Oh, no problem," I said. "Thank you for being my friend."

She smiled again and shook her head. "That's why I like you. You're just so laid back."

She obviously didn't know me that well. I liked to think of myself as being laid back and I usually was, but since she and Carrie had become "friends" I was nuttier than a fruit cake. But I decided then and there to stop having trouble with it. I would take it for what it was and be glad I had it.

"It's hard to meet people who just don't want to use you for your money and all that shit," she said. "And I don't have a problem giving things to people; I want to give things, it's just…you wonder if they like you or your money. With you and Carrie, I know you like *me*."

I would have liked her if she had come to the house barefooted. Or naked. In fact, that would have been very nice.

"We like you, Veronica," I said. "And you don't have to worry about *anything* with us."

"I know that," she said and smiled happily. "It's so hard to find true friends, and not just for me but for everyone in the world and I just feel blessed that I have two really good friends in my life. I care about you both, you know? I really do."

"We care about you."

She smiled again. "Thanks, Clark."

We smiled at each other for a moment until Carrie came into the room and told us that dinner was ready.

She turned to her and said, "Thank you, Carrie."

Carrie eyed her, then me and said, "No problem."

We had lobster tails for dinner and afterwards, Veronica suggested we take, "A dip in the Jacuzzi."

So we took a dip.

It didn't take them any time at all to get started. They were naked already and just started splashing water at each other playfully and after a minute or so of that, Veronica grabbed Carrie and pulled her over to her. She cupped her chin and pulled her lips to hers and they kissed.

I sat there dumbstruck. I had forgotten how nice it was to see this live. I could sit and watch forever. But doing was so much better than watching.

They pulled apart and slid over to me and each put a hand on my dick, which was so hard it throbbed. I kissed Carrie for a moment and then I went to Veronica and kissed her. I rotated my mouth and tongue between them until Carrie sat on top of me and we began to fuck. Veronica kept kissing me and fondling Carrie's breasts. A few times she pulled away and kissed them, sucking on her nipples until Carrie threw her head back and moaned.

I began to pump into Carrie and she pushed back, splashing water everywhere. Veronica kept kissing me and put her hand on Carrie's clit, which made her ride me harder. I grabbed her ass and started fucking her harder and we came at the same time.

We got out of the tub and Carrie pushed Veronica down on the floor, climbed on top of her and they wrapped their legs around each other's and began to hump. I just sat there and watched until they came and I got hard again.

I went over to them and stood over Veronica, who rose up and grabbed my dick and began to suck me, hard. Carrie got between her legs and began to eat her out, slurping and licking her wet and swollen pussy until Veronica gave a cry and started humping her face, grinding her hips in circles until she came and then I came again.

We kept at it for a very long time, each of them taking a turn with my dick and then they would go back to each other every time they got me off. They were insatiable. And I began to love them, and I mean really love, them. They were so different yet so alike they went together perfectly. I wondered briefly what I would do if they ever wanted to stop all this. I would miss it, that's for sure.

We fell asleep on Veronica's big bed wrapped in each other's arms. I didn't think life could get any better than this. I was wrong.

Veronica moves in.

The next day, I was walking down the hall at work and saw Arthur. Before I could stop myself, I gave him a good-natured slap on the back and said, "Yo!"

I guess I was just in a really good mood. He glared at me and I immediately regretted saying anything to him. I had forgotten about him coming by the house. And, I guess, that meant we weren't friends anymore. Hell, I liked Veronica a helluva lot better than him anyway. So, if this meant losing him as a friend, then that's what it meant. Any man would have picked Veronica. And if he didn't, he wasn't much of a man.

He pushed my hand off his arm in disgust and hissed, "Yo, yourself!"

"Huh?" I asked and grew embarrassed.

"Listen, ass," he said. "I know what's up!"

"'What's *up*?" I asked. "And what is *up*?"

"It's got nothing to do with you," he said, fuming. "Or your good old boy accent, either!"

What was he getting at?

"Excuse me?" I asked.

"She's not after you, bud; she's after your wife!"

"That's crazy!"

"No, it's the truth. I've seen the way they act. Soon they'll get tired of you and run off together and you'll be sitting on your ass cursing yourself because you let it happen!"

"What the hell are you talking about?"

He leaned in close and said, "Haven't even thought about it, have you?"

"About what?"

"About the two of them," he said. "They might let you watch or whatever, Clark, but they only like each other."

Damn him anyway! I thought I had gotten all that shit out of my head and here he was putting it right back in. I decided to set him straight.

"Look, what we have is..." I stopped and nodded at a few co-workers as they passed, then stepped to him and whispered, "Look, we have a nice thing is all. A once in a lifetime thing. It's just curiosity."

"No, it's more than curiosity. I mean, look at me, I'm a nice looking guy, a little hefty, sure—"

Denise, the receptionist, passed and said, "I'll say."

"Well, yeah, fuck you, Denise!" he yelled after her. "Is the whole office interested in everything I do?!"

Absolutely not. No one really gave a shit about him, the poor bastard. They just liked to give him hell.

"Arthur, you have to understand, it's nothing more than mere curiosity. Experimentation."

I shook myself. Where the hell did that come from? It sounded like something out of a sex education book.

"Yeah and why are you the lucky guy? You know what? I don't care. But if I were you, I d have a long talk with my wife. Other than that, you can go fuck yourself."

He started off. I considered what he just said for half a second and decided he was full of shit.

He turned and said, "Oh, if you see Veronica, tell her I said hi."

I raised one eyebrow at him. He *was* crazy. Like I would do that anyway! But I couldn't help but take what he said into consideration. What if…

Oh, shit, here it was again.

When I got home, Carrie was in the kitchen cooking spaghetti. Another favorite. Between all the sex and good food, I was living high on the hog. I liked the feeling, too. However, I didn't feel deserving of it. I just knew there was a catch. What was the catch? Not knowing was starting to drive me mad. I hadn't really thought about it until Arthur had started his shit but now I couldn't get it out of my mind. No man was this lucky.

"Hello, there," I said and kissed the back of her neck.

"Bonjour," she replied and smiled at me. "Spaghetti. I thought I should try to it make again."

"Yeah, the last time was a disaster."

"I thought I could make it good," she said and nodded. "I didn't know it bubbled! How was I supposed to know this?"

I chuckled and remembered coming home to a kitchen that was covered in spaghetti. She had tuned it on high and left it uncovered. It had boiled and bubbled and splattered everywhere, even on the ceiling. It took forever to clean up.

"So…" I began and walked to the table and sat down. "Would you sit down for a minute?"

She gave it one more stir, came to the table and said, "Spaghetti is Veronica's favorite."

"She's not here, is she?"

"Oh, if she should be, what would you do?"

She leaned over and nuzzled my neck seductively. I wanted to throw her down right then and there and fuck her brains out, but I also wanted to talk. It was an odd choice. For me or any man. Talk? Sex? Talk. Didn't make much sense but I'd go with it.

"Listen, Carrie—"

She pulled back and stared into my eyes. "We have fun, don't we, darling?"

"Yes, it is very fun, but we need to talk."

"Oui?" She kissed my cheek and went back to the stove.

"It's just such a good thing" I said. "But Arthur mentioned—"

"Arthur!" she yelled and turned on me, brandishing a wooden spoon. "If I hear his name one more time in this house!"

I held up my hands and said hurriedly, "I know, but, he said—"

"You give a shit what that pig says?!" she spat. "You should never listen to that pig!"

I shrugged.

"Never!" She hit the counter with the wooden spoon for emphasis. "Arthur is a pig!"

One thing about Carrie, when she didn't like someone, she really, really didn't like them. There was no gray area for her. She either liked or she hated. In Arthur's case, she hated. And, don't get me wrong, I could see her point. He was crass and somewhat odd, but he had made a very valid point. Like I said, there was no way this could last and I didn't want to lose Carrie just so I could get a little threesome action. I didn't like the thought of losing Veronica, either, but the longer she stayed around, the harder it would be to let her go.

"This is not about Arthur," I said and walked over to her. "The point is I think maybe you are developing an *attraction* to her—to Veronica. Maybe?"

She stared at me like I was crazy before she turned back to the stove. "Of course I am attracted to her. She is a very good friend."

"Oh, I understand. You're lonely."

"No, not lonely." She considered. "I am…how do you say…"

"Scared? Frightened? Anxious?"

"No." She shook her head. "I am very much… I like her very much."

"But, really, what is this all about?" I asked and leaned back to watch her face.

"What?"

"This ménage a trois."

"Oh!" she squealed and slapped her hands together. "Your French is improving!"

"You know what I mean, Carrie."

"It's fun, nice is all. No big deal. I've done it in the past, have you not?"

"I should be so fucking lucky!"

"Then you take it for what it is, darling," she said.

"And what is it?"

"Fun for us."

We smiled at each other. So that's all it was. Fun. Fun for me and fun for her. I could handle that.

"I just wanted to make sure," I said and clapped my hands together. "So where is our fun girl?"

She turned back to the stove. "Oh, she went to get her things."

"Her things?"

"She lost the lease on her apartment," she said. "She's moving in with us."

I almost passed out.

· · ·

But who was I to argue?

I mean, *come on*. Two beautiful women who got along great with each other living under the same roof as me and allowing me to fuck them senseless? I was one lucky bastard. I wasn't about to fuck that up.

It didn't take any time to settle into a routine.

They were so hot. They would get ready in the mornings together, helping one another with their hair and make-up. I would just watch from the sidelines. I loved watching them get ready. Sometimes they would shower together and there was always a lot of giggling and teasing. And a lot of touching and a lot of soaping up firm bodies. Sometimes they allowed me to shower with them. Those mornings were the best. The other mornings weren't anything to scoff at, either.

After we were finished getting ready, we would all go into the kitchen and prepare breakfast. Nothing fancy, usually just an egg and some toast and coffee. We would sit at the table and talk as we ate. It was almost as if we were a little family.

They would see me to the door, each of them taking turns kissing me. I think we got a few looks from the neighbors but I really didn't care. Then I was off to work. I have no idea what they did during the day but they would be waiting on me when I got home.

Sometimes we went out for dinner but most days Carrie and Veronica pitched in and cooked a fabulous meal. We would eat and discuss our days, and then we would all help clean up. After that, we would head to the living room and watch some TV. It wouldn't take long before the long looks between Veronica and Carrie started and it would only be a matter of time before we were all on the floor going at it.

I was so happy, I was beside myself.

Sometimes they waited until we were all in bed together. Then they would start caressing me. Little fingertip touches at first, some nibbling on my chest and ears and lips. One of them would climb on top of me or they would both get on their knees and suck me off. Once when we were lying in bed, they each took one of my legs and while yanking me off they humped my legs and got off as I got off. I took turns kissing each of them. That was one of the best times.

They also liked to get out the vibrators and Veronica even purchased a huge ten inch rubber cock. The first time she used that thing on Carrie I was yanking myself so hard I was sure I would pull my dick off. And when Carrie turned it on her…let's just say, I was exhausted by the night's end.

And we would all fall asleep, content and happy. And we'd start the next morning out as the others had started.

It was a good life, if I say so myself. And I do. Say so.

The resident dick.

As I was leaving work a few weeks later, Arthur fell in step beside me and said, "Oh, hello, Lesbian Man."

"Excuse me?" I asked.

"Heard Veronica moved in with you guys."

I stopped walking. "Where did you hear that?"

"Veronica."

I eyed him.

"I tracked her down, so what?"

"How did you do that?" I asked.

"I followed her," he said and added, "But I wasn't stalking or anything. Not really."

Oh, not really. What an asshole. What would it take with this guy? A fucking restraining order? Jail time?

I started walking again and said, "Is there something you want, Arthur?"

"Yeah, there is one thing. Your life."

I rolled my eyes.

"But really, I just wanted to see how it was going."

"It's going fine," I said. "And stay out of it."

"I will," he said. "I will."

I stopped walking and said, "I am the happiest man alive and I don't need someone like you passing judgment on me."

"I'm not passing judgment. I'd be the resident dick with those two any day."

I eyed him. "I am *not* the resident dick."

"Yeah, you are."

I calmed myself before I could get frustrated and angry. "Look, Arthur, it's not every man that can say he has two beautiful women at his beck and call."

As soon as the words were out of my mouth, I remembered that last night we were watching TV and Carrie asked for some popcorn. I had gotten up to make some and when I came back in with a big bowl, Veronica said, "What? No sodas?" So I had to rush back to the kitchen and get some sodas while they just sat there. It was almost as if I was a servant or something.

Not that I had a problem with it, but Carrie had called me a scatterbrain. And then, she asked for a foot rub and Veronica asked for a back rub. I didn't get either from them, but then again, it had led to some really, really hot sex, so what's the big deal? So what if I was at their beck and call? At least I got to have sex with them.

But then...

I stared at Arthur. What if he was right and they were really in love with each other and they were just keeping me around as the resident dick? All of a sudden, I felt panic. I tried to stop it but it came anyway. I felt like I was going to explode. My heart began to race and I began to sweat and...

"I gotta go," I told him and rushed off.

I took off in a hurry and looked around for my Marta station. I had to park in a lot and then take the Marta in. I hated it but I couldn't afford the parking downtown. I found my station, got on my train and sat down.

I sat there for a few moments and cleared my head. I looked up and noticed that something was off. All of the passengers on the train were women. And not just everyday average women but gorgeous, out of this world beautiful women.

What the fucking hell was going on?

I shook my head and stared up at an ad on the ceiling of the train. It was of two gigantic pails of milk.

What the...?

I took a breath and stared at my shoes.

"I fucked her."

I jumped and turned. A woman had sat down next to me.

"What did you say?" I asked.

She looked at me like I was crazy and snapped, "I didn't say anything."

I was losing my mind.

"Sorry," I mumbled. I glanced at the two pails of milk, sighed and sat back and closed my eyes. When I opened them again, the pails of milk had turned into two gigantic breasts. I shook my head and it was two pails of milk again.

I was losing my mind.

The ride usually only took about ten minutes. Today it seemed to take forever. How long had I been on here? I stared at my watch. Oh, about five minutes. Another five to go, then I'd get in my car and go home. Everything would be okay.

I looked out the window and blinked. In the reflection, all of the women were in their skivvies. That couldn't be right. I turned back to them. They were in their clothes. I looked back at the window and they were once again in their skivvies. I looked back at them in the train. Clothes. In the window, skivvies. In the—

Ah, fuck it!

I wiped at my sweaty brow. The women began to move around the train and rubbed up against me as they passed. I curled inwards to make myself as small as possible.

"Hi, I'm Sally. Carrie and I met two years ago."

I jerked around. "Who said that?"

The women gave me looks. I looked back out the window. They were still in their skivvies. I knew it was all in my head but the whole thing was beginning to really freak me out. How could I imagine that?

"Hello, I'm Jennifer and Veronica and I had an on-again, off-again relationship a year ago."

I looked around. They were minding their own business. *I was losing my mind!*

"I met Carrie and Veronica two days ago," someone whispered in my ear. "You can guess the rest."

I squeezed my eyes shut and shook my head. The train finally stopped. I jumped up and ran out. I didn't stop until I got to my car. And I put the pedal to the metal all the way home and there I ran into the house. It was quiet and no one was around.

They were gone.

I realized I was covered in sweat and my head was pounding inside my head. I felt awful. But that didn't stop me from looking around and yelling for them.

"Carrie! Veronica! Where are you?!" I yelled and ran through all the rooms.

They weren't here. They were gone. They had left me. I knew it was too good to be true.

I sat down on the couch and put my head in my hands. Not a minute later, I heard the front door open and Carrie and Veronica came in loaded down with grocery bags. They were chattering about something and seemed to be in a good mood.

I was so happy to see them I almost cried.

They stopped and stared at me. Carrie rushed over, dropping the grocery bags in the process. "Clark, what is wrong?"

Veronica stared at us, her eyes wide.

She touched my face. "He's in a cold sweat, Veronica!"

"Are you okay, Clark?" Veronica asked before she sat beside me and took my hand.

Phew. They were here. I wasn't losing my mind. I just had a panic attack and things got a little freaky. That's all. I couldn't let them know, either. They would think I *was* crazy. I would keep it all to myself and pray it never happened again.

"No," I said. "I think what I had for lunch made me sick."

"Poor baby," Veronica said and kissed my cheek.

She and Carrie stared at each other. Carrie smiled at her, then at me. I smiled back.

"You okay now?" Veronica asked.

Actually I was still a little shaken. I willed myself to say, "No, I'm cool. I mean, I actually started having these weird thoughts about the two of you leaving and…"

I stopped myself. I sounded so pathetic.

"We would never leave you, darling," Carrie said and touched the side of my face.

"Oh, I know," I said. "It's just the… You know, being sick you have all these weird thoughts and…"

"We're not going anywhere, Clark," Veronica said and rubbed my back. "Everything's okay."

"Oh, I know," I mumbled. "I know that."

Carrie said, "We'd never leave you, love."

That was such a good thing to hear.

Mini-break.

"What do you mean you're leaving?!" I yelled from the bedroom doorway.

They glanced up at me and shrugged and went right back to packing their overnight bags.

"It's just for weekend," Carrie said.

"But why can't I go?" I asked.

"It's a chick thing, Clark," Veronica said.

"So?"

She studied me and shook her head. "Clark, it would just seem *weird* if you came with us."

"But, but—"

"It's just a mini-break," she said and waved her hand at me. "Just for us girls."

But it wasn't fair! I wanted to shout and jump up and down on the floor. *Take me with you!* Please?

"What am I supposed to do all weekend?" I demanded to know and crossed my arms. This was really pissing me off. First they tell me they would always be around and the next thing I know, they've got a trip planned to some fucking spa.

They shook their heads.

"Huh?" I asked, on the verge of more panic.

They ignored me.

"Listen!" I said. "Why don't you two stay here?"

"Because it's planned and paid for and we want to go," Veronica said.

"But, but—"

"But it's settled," Carrie said and slammed her suitcase shut.

Damn it.

An hour later they were packed and asked me to carry their bags out to their car. I almost told them to fuck off, but then I didn't. I picked up the fucking bags, which weighed a damn ton and loaded them into Veronica's trunk. I was still pissed off but now I was bordering on desperation.

They came out of the house with their arms linked. They looked so happy it made me sick. I leaned against the driver's door and waited until Veronica came over to open it. I didn't move.

"Get out of the way, Clark," she said.

I grumbled and moved. She eyed me and shook her head as she opened the door.

"Come on, let me go with you," I said.

Carrie stopped at the door of the car and said, "It will be boring for you. All mud wraps and massages; boys don't like those things."

"I could hang out by the pool."

"They don't have a pool," Veronica said.

Liar!

"What will I do all weekend?" I asked.

They glanced at each other and shrugged.

Carrie snapped her fingers. "I know! Go see that woman you know."

"What woman?" I asked.

"Your mother," she said and waved her hand.

"My mother is in Austin."

"Who's that other woman we visit?"

Oh, God, no. Nooooo! Not *her.* I didn't want to see *her.*

I said, "My aunt Meredith?"

She nodded. I shivered. I only saw my aunt Meredith occasionally and that was more than enough. She gave me the creeps. She was really, really old. In fact, she was my *great* aunt. She smelled funny, like mothballs, and had blue hair. She was the black sheep of the family. No one understood her and no one wanted to. But she didn't care. I might have looked up to her *if* she hadn't been so weird. She once gave me a hard pinch on my face that left a bruise. When I showed my mother, she shrugged and said, "She's just crazy. Stay away from her."

And I had. I had moved to New York, and then to Atlanta and the next thing I know, my mother called me and told me to go visit her. She had retired to Atlanta in some condo complex for senior citizens. So, I did my family duty about once a year.

"Bye, handsome," Veronica said and kissed me, then got into the car.

I stared after her and then at Carrie, "Come on, Carrie. I'm your husband. Take me with you."

"No," she said and gave me a peck on the cheek. "Have a nice weekend, love. We will see you on Sunday."

"But, but—"

She ignored me and got into the car without another word. Veronica gave one last wave and backed out of the drive. They disappeared down the street. I was all alone. Bitches! Well, fuck them. I could have fun without them. I'd show them a thing or two about having fun.

I thought about fun. What the hell did I do for fun? I had been married for so long I had no idea what to do by myself. I went back into the house and sat on the couch. I looked around the room. It seemed so empty without them. I cursed under my breath and finally picked up the phone and dialed.

"Hello! Aunt Meredith?" I said.

"Who's this?" she snapped.

I groaned.

My aunt Meredith gave me a tight smile as I entered her condo. She was dressed really young for her age, which was anybody's guess, and her hair was in rollers and covered with a scarf. I wondered if it was still blue.

We kissed hello and she sat me down in the living room and went for coffee. After she served me, we settled down, sipped our coffee and didn't speak for the longest time.

Finally she said, "How's Carrie?"

I nodded and smiled. "Good, thanks."

"And Veronica?"

I did a spit take. The coffee just came out of my mouth and flew all over her coffee table. She eyed me but ignored the mess.

"What was that?" I asked and sat up, scratching my neck.

"Veronica," she said. "How is she?"

"How do you…?"

"I ran into the girls a few weeks ago at that place…" She snapped her fingers. "What's it called?"

"Good Gourmet?"

"Yes! Good Gourmet!" she squealed as if were some big deal. "Didn't she tell you?"

I shook my head.

"They're such sweet girls," she said and sipped her coffee. "They took me out to lunch."

They did?

"And look at this outfit," she said and opened her arms. "They bought it for me."

I stared at it. She was dressed in a black tank top and a pair of jeans and looked totally ridiculous. She usually wore old house dresses because she was, in fact, an old lady and that's what old ladies were supposed to wear.

"Really?" I said.

She nodded. "I really like them."

I looked away from her. She and Carrie had hated one another on the spot. Carrie told me she thought Meredith was "odd" and "smelled funny". Now they were chummy. Weird.

"Did you know they were going away together?" I asked.

"To the spa?" she asked and picked up a cookie. "Of course. They asked if I'd like to tag along but I have a date."

"You have a *date*?"

She nodded proudly. "I do and with a very nice gentleman."

"Well, good for you," I said and sipped my coffee. I couldn't help myself; I had to ask, "Since when do you date?"

"Well, the girls told me I shouldn't be alone and set me up with a matchmaking service. It's worked out very well. I have several boyfriends now."

I just stared at her.

"Oh, look at the time!" she said and didn't even look at her watch. "I have to go."

Well, that was that. I set the cup down on the coffee table and stood.

"It was good to see you, Aunt Meredith," I said and kissed her cheek.

"You too, Clark," she said. "And be sure to tell the girls hello for me."

Like hell I would.

There had to be something to this Good Gourmet place. That's where Carrie and Veronica had met and then they saw my aunt in there. I was going to check it out. Maybe the place had some sort of love potion or something.

It was just a regular market with stuff from all over the world—vegemite and other odds and ends. It was a little too frou frou for me. I grabbed a basket and bought some chips and imported beer.

"Is that him?"

I turned to see Dave and Denise, two of my co-workers. Denise was the bitchy receptionist and Dave worked in claims. They had met on the job and were engaged to be married. Lucky them. They always walked around hand in hand and disgusted everyone with their little kisses and pet names, "sugar hon" and "sugar lump".

"It is!" Denise exclaimed and smiled at me. "Hey Clark!"

"Oh, hello!" I said and waved, then went back to studying a can of imported beer. I didn't want to talk to them. They were affable and everything but I wasn't at work and I didn't *have* to talk to them when I wasn't. Besides, I was still peeved from being abandoned.

They walked up to me and stopped. Shit.

I turned and said, "How's it going?"

"Fine," Dave said. "What are you doing?"

"Just picking up some things for the house."

"Doesn't your wife shop?" he asked.

"Yeah, she does. I guess she just forgot…" I waved the can of beer. "She's been busy."

"Yeah, I heard about that," Denise said.

I couldn't keep myself from squirming. "About what? She uh…she's been busy. She went out of town for the weekend."

"Oh, with her girlfriend?" she asked and gave me a sly smile.

Bitch!

"Excuse me?" I said and shook my head as if I didn't quite understand.

Another sly smile. "Oh, nothing. I just heard that you had a woman living with you."

"What's that?" I asked and played dumb. "Oh, you mean Veronica. She's the...ummm...live-in housekeeper."

They both raised their eyebrows at me.

I said, "Where did you hear that?"

"Arthur," Dave said. "He's spreading rumors about you around the office."

I chuckled, "Well, you know what they say about rumors..."

"No, what do they say about rumors?" Denise wanted to know.

I thought for a moment and came up with nothing. So I turned to Dave, "So, what are you two doing here?"

"Huh? Oh, well, we were just out doing a little shopping and then we're going to have a drink. Care to join us?"

Ummm...

An hour later, we were sitting in a nearby bar and grill. I lit a cigarette and gave Dave and Denise a tight smile. They had been telling me about the rumors, which consisted of being shacked up with two women. They told me about how everyone thought I was some sort of bigamist and/or pervert, though technically I wasn't because I was only married to one of them. The pervert part was a matter of opinion.

They were jealous, that's all. It pissed me off. I mean, it was none of their business what I did. What was it to them? Why don't people just mind their own fucking business?! The answer was right in front of my eyes, but I was too blind to see it: They didn't have much of a life.

"You heard this from Arthur, right?" I asked. "You know, he has an unhealthy attraction to Veronica."

"He's not the only one, is he?" Dave said and elbowed me.

I stared at him and got a gay vibe. I don't know why, but this guy just seemed so gay. He used a lot of flourish when he talked and he was always eyeing me at work. But I didn't know if he was gay, nor did I care.

"Well, I think it's sick, Clark," Denise said. "You're married!"

"Yes I am," I said. "But I never said I was living with two women. Veronica is my housekeeper."

"Bullshit," she said and shook her head.

"Obviously, you should look up the definition of housekeeper!" I drank the last of my beer and stood. "Maybe I'm not the only one with a sick mind. I mean the one with... Arghh! Fuck off!"

I stomped off, leaving them with their mouths hanging open.

I heard Dave say, "It's no wonder he's always so sleepy."

Denise gave him a slap. Served him right.

I stayed by myself all weekend with a case of beer. I ordered in pizzas and watched all the TV I wanted. I slept a lot, too. I was extremely rested when they came home late Sunday evening. The only odd thing that happened was this weird dream I had when I was napping on Sunday afternoon. In it, everyone at work had been harassing me about being shacked up with two women. It went on and on and on. And then someone set off the sprinkler system. Everyone took off their clothes and ran around naked. The next thing I know, my Aunt Meredith and I were driving around the country on riding lawn mowers. It was like we were in a race or something. She'd get a little ahead, then I'd get a little ahead and it went on forever. And my lawnmower kept breaking down.

Just like my piece of shit car. I really needed to trade that damn thing in.

"Clark?" Veronica said sweetly and kissed my cheek.

I had been napping when I heard her voice. I jerked awake and stared at her, then at Carrie. They certainly looked refreshed.

"How was your weekend, darling?" Carrie asked and sat down beside me.

"Oh, it was *great*," I said, laying in the sarcasm.

They looked around the living room which was trashed with pizza boxes and potato chip bags and beer cans.

"Looks like someone had a party," Veronica said.

"Yeah," I said. "But no one came."

The next morning I got up late. I rushed to the bathroom but stopped short when I saw Veronica. She was sitting on the side of the vanity shaving her legs. She was nearly nude and only had on a little tank top and a pair of panties. She looked divine. Carrie was nowhere to be seen.

"Shit!" she said and touched her leg.

I stared. She'd cut herself. She glanced up at me and smiled. I backed away from the door. I suddenly felt weird as if I shouldn't be staring at her like that when Carrie wasn't around.

"I cut myself," she said and pointed to her leg.

"Oh...too bad," I muttered.

She hopped down and came over to me. "Yeah, it hurts really bad."

I took another step back and said, "Sorry."

She touched my face and tip-toed for a kiss. I was about to kiss her but I felt wrong about doing it. I know I only felt wrong because of all those rumors at work. But it just didn't feel right. I didn't have any trouble when Carrie was around, but she wasn't here. And I felt like a louse. I was only punishing myself and I knew it. But I couldn't help myself.

I pulled back from her abruptly. She stared at me and a look of hurt came across her face.

I turned and said, "It's just...I've got to have some coffee."

She growled, "And a good kick in the ass."

And then she slammed the bathroom door in my face.

Aggressive today.

I was working diligently at my desk when Denise came in. "Mr. Baker wants to see you, Clark."

I looked up at her. "Excuse me?"

"You heard me," she snapped and left.

I groaned and got up. Mr. Baker was my boss and I rarely even saw him. I did my work and he left me alone. That was the unspoken agreement we had. Something had to be up.

When I got to his office, he was on the phone but motioned for me to sit down. I sat down and stared at the portly fellow. He was so damned old and worn looking. I could tell he was sexually frustrated, too. Men can't hide that. Why didn't he retire, hire a hooker and go on vacation? He had the money.

He was saying into the phone, "Yeah...okay. Look, I've got someone here. I said I'd be home! I said..." He shook the phone then got back on, "Yeah. YEAH!"

He slammed the phone down and regained his composure.

"You wanted to see me, sir?" I said.

"Yes, I did," he said. "Good to see you, Clark."

"And you," I said politely.

"How have things been going?" he asked.

"I had a little problem with a client the other day."

"Oh?"

"Nothing to worry about, though," I said and took a deep breath.

"Good, good," he said nicely.

I nodded nervously. "Mr. Baker, how can I help you?"

"I'm not going to beat around the bush."

Oh, shit. This can't be good.

"Clark, there has been some talk about...your home situation."

"Huh?"

"Some of the women—uh females— uh...ladies...uh...whatever the hell we're supposed to call them now have been complaining that you are...how do I say this?"

He paused and took a moment. I stared at him. This couldn't be good.

He continued, "That you're shacked up with two women."

"Mr. Baker, I—"

"Look, I am not going to fire you or reprimand you for things that are perfectly legal." He gave me a hard look. "It is legal, isn't it?"

I got so frustrated I could have exploded. "Of course it's legal! But I don't see what business it is of anyone's what I do when I'm not here. Whether or not I'm shacked up with anybody, which I'm not, sir...I mean..."

I gave up and put my head in my hands. I was screwed.

He said, "Technically, it isn't anyone's business what you do at home."

"Good," I said.

He leaned forward towards me. "Unless you…want to share…"

"Excuse me?"

He straightened up. "Oh, I understand if you don't want to. The females just wanted me to talk to you. They're a bit miffed is all. They think you're a pervert."

"I am not a pervert!"

He picked up a cigar and chewed on it. "That's nice to hear."

At least something I said was nice to someone's ears.

"How did you do it?" he asked, eyeballing me.

"What?" I asked even more frustrated.

"Oh, never mind. I'm just very jealous of you. I've got no problem admitting that either. What man wouldn't be?" He stared thoughtfully into space. "I remember once when I was in the Navy…"

Oh, good God.

I cleared my throat and said, "Sir?"

"That must be some wife you have." He winked. "But, anyway, who is the other woman?"

"She's my housekeeper!" I lied and was damned glad I had that option.

"Your housekeeper? Well, they told me…oh, shit, Clark, I apologize. People start talking and the next thing they've got you shacked up with two beautiful women." He paused. "I took one look at you and thought, hell no! How can *he* get two women? It's your

accent, that whole cowboy thing. But, yeah. Anyway…
Your housekeeper. Huh."

We stared at each other for a moment.

"I didn't know you could afford a housekeeper on
your salary," he said, and then added, "What cleaning
agency does she work for?"

Give me a fucking break.

I felt and looked like shit as I stumbled into the
house later that evening. Veronica and Carrie were on
the living room floor working a puzzle and smoking
cigarettes. They looked contented and happy. It really
pissed me off.

"Darling!" Carrie squealed and jumped up and ran
over to give me a kiss. "We're so happy to see you!"

Veronica smiled, got up and made me a scotch and
water. After she kissed me, she said, "You look so hot in
a suit!"

I grabbed the drink and downed it. "This is what I
fucking mean!"

I threw the glass against the wall and turned to
them. They stared at me like they couldn't believe I'd
just done that. I couldn't believe it myself. It just
happened. How weird. I guess that's what anxiety does
to you.

They didn't back off.

"He's aggressive today," Veronica said. "I like that."

She put her arms around my waist and Carrie got
behind her. As she kissed me, Carrie kissed her neck.

I pushed them away and said, "I can't do this anymore! You two are ruining my life."

Carrie said, "Pardon?"

I turned to her, "Carrie, it's just not normal!"

Veronica eyed me, and then turned to Carrie, then back to me. "What's not normal?"

"Us! We are not normal! This whole situation is ab-fucking-normal! Don't you get it? One man and two women are not supposed to live in perfect harmony!"

"What are you saying, Clark?" Veronica asked.

"I'm saying this whole situation is a little unusual."

"What is unusual?" Carrie wanted to know.

Veronica turned to her and said, "He means it isn't like what everyone else does."

"Oh," she said.

I groaned.

"I think I get the hint," Veronica said and started out of the room.

Carrie cried, "No, you don't go anywhere."

Veronica stopped and turned around with her arms crossed. She gave me a disgusted look. I looked away from her. Part of me felt bad, like I was betraying them. But the other part was pissed off, like they were betraying me by being so...available and hot and delicious.

Carrie pointed her finger in my face and said, "Tell me, Clark, why are you so unhappy? Everything was fine yesterday, now it's a different story!"

I nodded and fumed and decided to tell them. "I had a little talk with my boss today at work."

They glanced at each other.

I nodded. "Yeah! He wanted to know what was going on in my personal life. I told him Veronica was the housekeeper!"

"Hold your horses!" Veronica shouted. "He wanted to know what you do after you get off work?"

"YES!"

"Why?" she asked. "I mean, what business is it of his?"

"I guess my life is more interesting than his!" I plopped down on the couch. "There's been some talk—rumors—I suppose, about my living arrangement."

"Well, last time I checked, this was a free country," Carrie said.

Veronica added, "What people do in the privacy of their own homes is no one's business."

"But it's carrying over to work. Arthur must have said something—"

They both roared at the same time, "ARTHUR!"

I jerked back. "So?"

Veronica said, "So, he's trying to set you up."

I thought about that. Maybe that was what this was all about. Arthur's jealousy and his infatuation with Veronica, but... But. Damn it. I couldn't win. One minute I was fine and the next I was verging on hysteria. The situation was just too good to be true. But it wasn't Carrie and Veronica who had the problem, it was everyone else. How weird was that?

"Don't worry about him," Veronica said. "I'll take care of him."

I stared at her and shook my head. "No, don't worry about it. It's taken care of."

"Do you want me to leave, Clark?" Veronica asked.

Carrie screeched, "NO!"

"I asked Clark a question, Carrie," she said. "Clark?"

Of course I didn't want her to leave. I just didn't want all this trouble over her staying. I just wanted my cake and I wanted to eat it too, whatever the hell that meant.

"Honestly, no, I don't." I stared up at her, hoping I sounded convincing. "I mean it."

She said, "Then I'll take care of it."

· · ·

Two days later, Arthur slammed into my office and he looked like hell. His face was covered in red scratches. He looked like he'd been mauled by a pack of wildcats.

I stared at him, shook my head and said, "What happened to your face?"

"Oh, I'll tell ya!" he roared.

"Okay."

"Those bitches of yours poisoned me! Then they took me to a dike bar and *those* bitches beat me up!"

"What?"

"And I'm just warning you, they'll poison you too!"

"What are you talking about?" I asked and eyed him. He looked absolutely insane.

"Veronica invited me over for lunch yesterday," he fumed. "Like an idiot, I went. She and Carrie met me at the door dressed..." He trailed off as if he were relishing the memory. Then he jerked his head and stared at me. "Anyway, they looked hot. They fed me lasagna and wine. I felt really sleepy after that and the next thing I know, we're in the car."

Was he making this up?

"So, they tell me we're just going to a bar for a drink. Well, they didn't say it was a dike bar. They get me in there, get me loaded and the next thing I know, they're screaming that I'm trying to molest them!"

I could see it.

"These bull dikes beat the shit out of me and then they…disappeared."

"Who?" I asked.

"What?" he said and scratched at the back of his head.

"Who disappeared?"

"Those bitches of yours," he fumed. "Veronica and Carrie."

I considered that.

He stared at me keenly. "Well?!"

I sat up and said, "That's absurd!"

He pointed to his face. "Would I do this to myself?"

"You might."

"No, they're out for all mankind! They hate all men! You're next, Clark."

"I don't understand."

"You got any life insurance?"

"Yeah."

"Then you better watch your back!"

"But I don't understand—"

"Understand this: they poisoned me and they're after you next! I'm just giving you a warning. Watch your food."

I shook my head.

"Those bitches of yours are crazy," he said and left without another word.

I put my head in my hands. Here it was again. Just when everything was going smoothly, someone came in to screw it up again. I told myself to ignore what he'd just said, that he was one crazy motherfucker. But then...

Maybe he had a point. I mean, why me? Yeah, I know I was married to Carrie but... Well, that was the reason. But... They could just be stringing me along and when the right moment came, *BAM!* I'd be dead. Women can do things like that. But Veronica was rich and whatever measly little life insurance I had wouldn't buy her anything she was accustomed to. I wouldn't do Carrie much good, either.

But every night, Veronica made me a scotch and water in the same glass. Ummm... Why the same glass every night? Why...

Shit! This was so stupid! Those two wouldn't hurt a flea! But...yeah, they *had* set Arthur up. But, he had been spreading rumors so they might have done it in my defense. And that was kind of sweet and considerate. But they might be doing to see if they could get away with it and when they realized they could, they would try something with me.

But why would they want to hurt me?

It took me a minute to come up with a reason. They might be in love with each other and killing me would be easier than breaking it off. A clean break. Goodbye, Clark. Or maybe, they weren't going to kill me. Killing me would be a little extreme, even for this paranoid concoction. Maybe they were just going to leave me. Oh, shit. That would almost be worse.

I'd have to investigate this further. No, I would not. I would not go home in another bad mood. But what if…

Yeah. What if?

They were cooking when I came home, huddled over the kitchen table poring over a recipe book. I stood in the doorway and watched them for over a minute before they even noticed I was in the room.

"We need some chili powder," Veronica said and went to the cabinet and opened the door.

"Cumin, too," Carrie told her and pointed at the cabinet.

"Got it," she said and pulled the spices out. She turned and saw me and smiled. "Hey, good looking!"

Carrie stared over at me and said, "Hello, darling."

"Hello. Ummm…" I stared around cautiously.

"Hungry?" Carrie asked.

I went to the cupboard and got some crackers. "No, I'll just have a cracker, thanks."

They stared at me and shrugged, then went back to the book. I watched them. Veronica sighed, picked up a bottle of something green and took it to the pot.

I intercepted it and held it back. "What is this?" I sniffed it. "Oh, God, it's rank!"

She grabbed it out of my hand, narrowed her eyes and said, "It's jalapeno pepper. For the chili."

"Oh," I said.

She shook her head.

"But it's green."

She turned to Carrie and gave her a curious look.

"Those peppers are green and a little stinky," Carrie said.

Oh.

"Are you okay, Clark?" Veronica asked.

"Fine," I said. "Just had a long day."

They glanced at each other and back at me.

"I'll just be on the couch if you need me," I said and went into the living room, sat down and turned on the TV. I fell asleep almost immediately.

"Clark?"

I jerked awake. Veronica was sitting next to me.

"Oh, Veronica," I said and sat up.

"How was work?" she asked.

"Fine, I suppose."

"Look, I know you probably spoke with Arthur."

"What?"

"All we did was give him a warning," she said. "He was getting out of control."

I eyed her but decided to play dumb, which I was good at. "I have no idea what you re talking about."

"You don't?" she smiled. "Well, good."

She slapped my knee just as Carrie came in pulling on a jacket.

"Where are you going, Carrie?" I asked.

"To my mother's."

"Your mother lives in France."

She considered. "Oui."

She left without another word. Well.

Veronica turned to me and smiled. "It's just me and you tonight."

I cleared my throat. She winked and loosened my tie. I just sat there and let her. When she had it undone, she threw it over her shoulder.

"Would you like a scotch and water?" she asked sweetly.

I shrugged. Sure, why not?

I watched as she got up and sashayed over to the little bar. Her ass was so nice and I appreciated a nice ass. It almost made me forget what a disaster my life was becoming. And that she was the main cause of it.

A moment later, she bought the drink back, sat down and kissed my cheek. "I know we haven't really had a chance to get know each other—one on one—so we're going to spend some quality time together tonight."

My eyes widened.

"Alone."

I cleared my throat and looked away. She cupped my chin and brought my face to hers and kissed me, first nibbling at my lips before slipping her tongue into my mouth. It felt so good, so right, but then it didn't.

I pushed her away and stood up.

She sighed like she was getting annoyed. "What's eating you? Now."

"I can't do it," I said. "I can't cheat on my wife."

"We've done it before."

"But she was in the room!"

"And? She cheats on you all the time."

My mouth dropped. "She does?!"

She rolled her eyes and said, "What do you think we do all day while you're at work?"

"All day?"

She laughed a little and said, "Just kidding, not all day, anyway."

I shook myself. This was a little too much. It just felt like a trap of some kind.

"Why are you so bothered?" she asked.

"Because I wouldn't feel right sleeping with you without Carrie being here."

"She does it!"

"It's not the same thing." I lit a cigarette and puffed on it for a good minute. She just sat there and watched me. We didn't say anything but I could feel that this was headed somewhere.

She sighed, got up and took my cigarette and put it out. "It is the same thing, Clark. All couples hit their peak and need extra-curricular activities."

"Look, our sex life was fine before you came around."

"Maybe for you it was," she said knowingly.

"What does that mean?"

She shrugged and went back to the couch.

I stomped over to her and said as calmly as I could, "I want you to tell me what you meant."

"By what?"

"That couples hit their peaks and all that crap! Is Carrie cheating on me?"

"Clark, it was a joke," she said. "I meant Carrie and I have sex when you're not here. You need to clean the wax out of your ears."

I grunted.

"You've been acting weird lately," she said. "Tell me what's wrong."

She motioned for me to sit. I didn't. I began to pace in front of her. I finally organized my thoughts and said, "Don't you think this living arrangement is a bit…abnormal?"

"You just love that word. Abnormal." She sighed and shook her head. "You're already said it a gazillion times tonight."

We stared at each other. I looked away first.

She sighed and said, "Maybe to some it would be 'abnormal'. I'm bisexual, so is Carrie. And you're…well, a man."

That's all I was, too.

She rolled her eyes. "How long did you and Carrie know each other before you got married?"

"Not very long," I said.

"What do you mean by that?" she asked.

"Well, it wasn't planned."

"But you're still together, right?"

I swallowed hard and said, "I suppose."

"Then leave it at that."

"Is Carrie going to be upset about this?" I asked.

"Who do you think suggested it?"

I turned to her and said, "Who are you, Veronica?"

She stared into my eyes for a long moment and then cracked up. "Geez! What is this? *Unsolved Mysteries?* Come on, Clark!"

I didn't crack up like she wanted me to. I didn't even crack a smile. I was so tense I could have jumped out of my skin. And over what? I didn't really know anymore. I was more confused now then when this whole thing started. I was over analyzing, that's all, but I couldn't stop. I was having obsessive thoughts. This was something good, very, very good and I should be overjoyed about it. But I knew there was a catch. There had to be a catch. What was the catch?

"Come on," she said softly. "Tell me what's wrong."

I feigned indifference and said, "Nothing. I'm just a little tired from work and..."

She looked at me like she didn't believe me and touched my arm. I jerked it back. She gasped a little and turned away, a look of hurt on her face.

Why had I done that?

"Listen," she said with just a trace of animosity, like she was holding it in. "It wasn't my idea to have a night alone with you. It was Carrie's, okay?"

I nodded.

"You know, Clark, for someone who has it so good, you sure do act stupid about it."

I knew that!

"And I don't want to spend a night with you anyway," she hissed and stood up. "I mean why the hell would I want that?"

I stared up at her. She glared back down and started out of the room. She stopped and turned around, her eyes blazing. I was almost scared. I had never seen her angry before. But that's what rejection does to women. It pisses them off. I shouldn't have rejected her.

"What do you think of me?" she snapped.

"Uh, well—"

"Don't fuck around with me," she hissed. "You think I'm some kind of home wrecker, don't you?"

"No, it's not that. It's—"

"That's what you think, I know it is. Well, let me tell you one thing, it was *your* wife who came on to me, okay? I had never even touched another woman before her. And it was *your* wife who invited me here to live with you."

"Veronica—"

"You're a son of a bitch," she said, simmering.

"It's just—"

"Zip it!" she hissed and held up one hand.

I stared at her. She was really pissed off. Though she was short, she looked ten feet tall right then. I stepped out of her way before she turned on me again.

"And let me tell you another thing, you cocksucker, no man in his right mind who is in your shoes right now would be whining about it. You've got a lot of nerve to come home acting all crazy!"

She was right. She was so right. I felt like shit then. Real shit. It wasn't her fault the people at work were giving me hell. It wasn't Carrie's either. And I was lucky. But with luck comes responsibility.

"I'm sorry," I said and walked over to her. "I really am."

I laid my hand on her arm. She jerked away and slapped me. Her eyes were brimming with fire. She was so pissed off she could have spit.

"Well," I said and rubbed my jaw.

"You deserve a lot worse," she said and started out of the room.

"Wait a minute!" I yelled and grabbed her arm again.

She turned and began to swat at me at me. Her arms were all over the place. I grabbed them and put them behind her back. She kept struggling and let out a stream of curses that would have made a sailor blush.

"Youcocksuckingsonofabitch!" she spat. "*GET OFF ME!*"

"Calm down and listen to me," I said and held her as still as I could. "I want—"

She got an arm free and popped me in the jaw. I almost saw stars. I shook my face and turned back to her. Her nostrils were flaring and she was seething and...

She looked so damned sexy.

I pushed myself onto her and forced my tongue into her mouth. She kept struggling but then gave in and began to kiss me back. She began to bite at me, ripping my shirt off my back and jerking my pants down. I ripped her shirt off and grabbed her breasts in both hands. I bent down and began to devour them, sucking on them until they were red. I sucked on her erect nipples until she cried out and grabbed me by the head and pulled me back to her mouth.

We kissed all the way to the couch and there she turned around. Ah, yes! She wanted it doggie.

She told me to, "Fuck me hard."

I ran my hands up and down her ass, then between her ass cheeks. She moaned and began to squirm. I grabbed onto her pants and pulled them off in one swift motion. I tore the panties from her body. She was now naked before me, her swollen pussy staring me right in the eye.

I bent down and began to eat it. She moaned again and moved against my face, purring my name. I sucked on her pussy and then began to finger her. She was so wet my fingers slid right in. I moved them around and placed my finger on her clit. That made her really purr. I loved that sound coming out of her mouth. She began to rock against me, shoving it in and around my face, making it slide around until she gave another gasp and screamed, "OHYEAHHHHHhhhhhhhh!"

"Now I'm going to fuck you," I said and shoved my cock into her.

She gasped. "Oh, yeah, Clark, don't stop."

"Like that?" I asked.

"Yeah," she moaned.

I grabbed her by the hair and pulled her up to me. "Harder?"

"Harder!"

I rammed into her harder. She began to shake and shimmy and moan even louder.

"I could fuck you all night," I told her.

"Fuck me all night," she moaned. "But do it hard."

I gave her another good thrust and she bucked up against me. She was coming again and she was coming hard. I had seen her do this before but this time it was different. She was the only woman in the room and I could fully concentrate on her, on her moving and sweating and looking so hot and sexy. I wanted to eat her up she looked so good.

I began to feel myself start to come. And it was a big one on the way. My whole body began to tense. I rammed into her, wanting it to last forever, knowing it couldn't but being glad it was her that was taking it and she was taking it all. She liked it hard. I liked giving it to her.

As I came, I gave her ass a good slap and that sent her over the edge. She was nearly trembling. I was trembling. There was nothing we could do about it but hold on and hope it lasted.

But it didn't. When it was over, I fell onto her back and held her tight and decided that no matter what happened I was going to tell the rest of the world to fuck off. This was where I always wanted to be. With her and with Carrie, knowing they were mine. Knowing I was the luckiest man in the world and I would just have to accept that responsibility.

She took me to a strip club to make up for "Slapping the shit" out of me.

I went along happily. The strippers eyed us and a few even winked at her. I smiled. I liked being with a woman who strippers dug.

We got a table near the back, ordered a couple of drinks and stared at the stage. After a few minutes, I said, "And why did we come here?"

"Well," she said. "Just something different to do. You don't like strip clubs?"

"No, it isn't that," I said and lit a cigarette. "It's just…"

"What?" she asked and smiled at me.

"Nothing."

She nodded and smiled at a pretty redheaded stripper, who smiled and winked back.

Veronica said, "She's cute, isn't she?"

I nodded.

"Maybe we could invite her over sometime and have a foursome."

Of course, I had been taking a sip of my drink and as soon as she said that, I nearly choked. She patted me on the back and kissed my cheek.

"You okay?" she asked sweetly.

I nodded. "I'm fine."

"Good," she said and smoothed the hair out of my eyes. "You need a haircut."

"You know," I said, staring her head in the eye. "You're not like any girl I've ever known."

She ruffled my hair and gave me that little, *you've got to be kidding me look* she had. "You don't get out much, do you?"

"I guess not."

She stood and said, "I'm gonna go tip."

I watched her approach the stage where about four men were waiting for their turn to tip the stripper. As she waited for the stripper to get to her, all the men checked her out. That kinda pissed me of but made me feel good at the same time. The stripper came over to her, ran her hands through her hair and bent down, pressing her tits in her face. She blushed and watched the stripper as she gyrated on the stage in front of her. She leaned back, held up her garter and Veronica slipped a dollar bill into it. They kissed each other's cheeks and she came back to the table as all the men in the place ogled her.

After she settled back in her seat, I said, "I've been meaning to ask you, and don't take this the wrong way, but, how long do you plan on staying?"

"Oh, just another hour or so then we can go home."

"No. I mean with Carrie and me."

"Do you want me to leave, Clark?"

"No, it's just…things are getting complicated." I took a breath. "It's just I don't want to…I hate to say this, but I don't want to commit and then you leave. I mean things are complicated enough as they are without…"

I nodded until she nodded back. I think she understood what I was saying.

"Let me tell you about things, Clark, they're only as complicated as you allow them to be."

She had a point.

"If you let other people run your life, then they will. But don't go bitching when you find they don't always want to do what's right for you."

I looked away.

"If you want me to go, then tell me to leave, Clark. I won't stay where I'm not wanted."

"I don't want you to go and I know Carrie doesn't either."

"Then what's the problem?"

"Nothing," I said. "I'm just being stupid."

"You need to stop that," she said and smiled.

"One last question."

"Okay," she said.

"Why me? I mean, why Carrie?"

"Why not? Why does there always have to be why?"

Yeah. *Why?*

She lit a cigarette and waved it in the air as she talked, "As I said, I haven't always liked other girls. It's just Carrie has a certain quality. She's feels the same way. She told me she's had sex with a few girls but never thought that she would…"

She stopped and looked away.

"Tell me," I said.

She turned back to me and said, "I never felt like this for another woman. Men, sure, sometimes, but not like I feel for her."

"How do you feel about her?"

"Let's just say I really, *really* like her," she said and smiled. "I don't know if it's love or what it is and I don't want to name it cause once you give something a name, you gotta feed it and worry about it and hope it never leaves you."

"You have a point."

"I mean, this is a once in a lifetime shot. To be with two people at the same time who you really care about? Wow. No one ever gets that."

I nodded. "I wonder why sometimes."

"Why what?"

"Why situations like ours don't happen more. I just wonder."

"Maybe they do but no one hears about it."

"Maybe," I said.

"But you don't have to wonder," she said. "It's because most people don't allow it to happen. They're scared. What will the neighbors think? All that shit. And so they try drugs and alcohol or whatever but that shit just numbs you."

"Yeah."

"The really good feelings are already there. No one ever taps into them because they're inhibited or whatever."

I nodded.

"But I'm not inhibited and neither is Carrie. Neither are you, if you'd just admit it."

"I admit it," I said.

She smiled and took a drag off her cigarette.

I said, "Quite the philosopher, aren't you?"

"Yeah, I talk shit all the time."

We cracked up.

"I'm enjoying our time together," she said. "I hope you are, too."

I nodded. "I am. I really, really am."

"You'd be a fool not to."

She was right.

She gave me a sultry look and glanced down at my crotch, and then put her hand on it. I felt my dick jump to attention. It almost burned.

"I like fucking you," she whispered. "And I like fucking her and I don't see a fucking problem with any of it."

I nodded and she moved her hand a little. She unzipped my pants.

She whispered, "I'm not here to ruin your marriage or your life. I'm just here to get off."

We laughed and her hand was now on my dick. She rubbed it up and down, stroked it.

I took her hand away and said, "You shouldn't do that here."

"But I should," she said.

She put her hand back and stroked my dick. We stared at the stage at a lovely stripper who went by the name Jenny. I let her jerk me off and when I started to come, she bent down as if she has lost something on the floor and sucked it out of me. And no one noticed a thing.

Read it and weep.

It was a good life I was leading but very tiring. When we got home from the strip club, Carrie was waiting on us. She and Veronica hugged each other closely once we walked in the door and started kissing, which lead to me kissing them and we ended up having sex on the living room floor. They pretty much wore me out the first time, then they kept me up all night fucking and then they fucked each other while I sat back and watched, smoking cigarettes. I don't even know what time I fell asleep.

I had just fallen asleep at my desk when Arthur charged in and threw a newspaper down on my desk.

Not him again.

He said, "Read it and weep, buddy!"

"What?" I asked and rubbed my face.

"Read it and weep," he said. "That's the society page."

The *what?*

Before I could pick the paper up, he grabbed it and began to read, "'*Ms. Chambers to donate funds to beautify city parks*' Can you believe that?!"

"Believe what?" I asked and yawned.

He went back to the paper, "'After her stay here, Ms. *Veronica* Chambers plans to relocate to France sometime after the New Year.' See?"

I grabbed the paper and looked it over. Veronica had donated some money for a park. Big deal.

"Arthur, this thing is months old," I said. "I didn't even know Veronica then. Where did you get it?"

"I found it lying around my apartment."

I just stared at him.

He wadded the paper up and threw it over his shoulder. "They're gonna take care of you and then run off to the city of lightning!"

I groaned, "The City of Lights."

"Huh?"

"It's called the City of Lights," I said. "Paris?"

"Who cares what it's called?" he said. "Don't be a fool, Clark."

I just stared at him. Just when I had everything all settled in my mind, he stormed in with something new. It wasn't me that was paranoid and crazy. It was him. He wanted to take me along. But I had to get off this ride or it was going to do me in.

"You're just jealous, Arthur," I said. "That's what all of this has been about. *You're* the one trying to ruin my life, not them! *You're* the one trying to get me fired. *You're* the one spreading rumors. You can't stand that I have something like this and you don't."

I sat back and dared him to deny it.

"Well, yeah, it does piss me off," he said.

I was almost disappointed he didn't deny it. I was ready for a good fight.

"But I'm not jealous," he said. "Not anymore. Those chicks are gonna do you in!"

"No, they're not, Arthur," I said. "You're just paranoid. I'm a big boy and I can take care of myself."

"You're a foolish man, Clark. It's hard enough to trust one woman, but *TWO!?* You're out of your frickin' mind."

Yeah, maybe. But it was me, not him, living with two beautiful women. And it was me, not him, who went home and fucked all night long. And it was me, not him, who was having the time of his life. And he couldn't stand that. And I was getting tired of all his shit.

He said, "Have you ever considered that she might have offed her other husband?"

"Arthur, her husband was eighty-six years old."

"So?" he said. "She could have turned his machine off or something."

"She didn't," I said. "He died of natural causes."

"Well, he might have," he said. "But you won't."

"Listen," I said and pushed myself back from my desk. "I'm happy and I like what I have and you're just jealous that you don't have it, too."

"You're damned right I am," he said. "But you have to watch women. They're very devious."

I rolled my eyes and stood up. "Okay, okay, whatever, Arthur. But I like what I have right now and I won't do anything to jeopardize it."

"You're a fool, Clark."

"And a happy one at that."

He shook his head and turned on his heel and exited the office. I was glad to see him go. He was really beginning to get on my nerves.

As I turned onto my street later, I noticed something very odd. There was a huge 4x4 pickup sitting in my driveway. I stopped the car on the other side of the street and started at it. Who could it be? A plumber? An electrician? A pizza delivery man? Who the hell was it?

I sat there for a moment and thought about it. All of a sudden, the damn piece of shit car died. I cursed and cranked it. Nothing.

"Shit!" I cursed and got out and popped the hood.

I looked it over good. Nothing looked amiss. I checked the oil. It was fine. Who knew what the hell was wrong with this damn thing? I sighed and just then noticed that the battery cables were a little loose. I tightened them, got back in the car and cranked it. It turned over.

I was just about to put it in gear when out of the corner of my eye I saw some movement on my lawn.

I wheeled around and saw that Veronica was being lifted and slung over some big guy's shoulder. Carrie stood to the side and laughed.

What the fuck?! Who was this fucker? He was a huge fucker, at least six-something and very…menacing. He looked like one mean motherfucker. Dark hair and big arms and… WHO THE FUCK WAS HE!?

Veronica and the guy played around a little, he put her down and then they walked—hand in fucking hand—to his truck. As he got in, she leaned against the door, smiling up at him. Carrie joined her and smiled at him, too. It was as if they were best friends or something.

Oh, good God.

He started the truck and Carrie and Veronica backed away from it, smiling and waving. He gave one wave, backed out of the drive and squealed his tires on the asphalt before he flew out of sight.

It dawned on me. It came at me so quickly I almost fell out of the car. Don't jump to conclusions. Don't jump to conclusions! But I did. I jumped and realized Arthur could very well be right.

No man was ever lucky enough to have two beautiful women at the same time! No man! Sure, they said they this and they said that, but in the end when I was a dead man, what would any of that matter? The clues were all there. Carrie and Veronica spent a lot of time alone together. Who knows what they came up with? They were both very smart. And they could get any man in the world to off me and be free as fucking birds.

But why would they want to off me? I took that into consideration. I really did. Although I couldn't come up with anything, it just made sense.

And now I had my proof that they were up to something. And the son of a bitch drove a 4x4 pickup. What kind of man drives a truck like that? A thug, a redneck, a... I stopped. I had wanted a 4x4 but Carrie had insisted on the Audi. Nevertheless, I wanted to kill him. How dare he come into my world and…? Were they lovers? Was that what they did all day when I was at work? Invited Mr.4x4 over and had a wild time?

Bitches. I'd get to the bottom of this thing if it was the last thing I ever did. And it very well might be.

As we were eating dinner, scenarios kept playing in my mind. Who was this fucker? He had to be the other man. He had to be! I knew something was going on! I knew that—

"You're quiet," Carrie said to me.

I jerked and stared at her. She smiled slightly and stared at the chicken on her plate, then back at me.

"Yeah, Clark," Veronica said, sipping her wine. "Another bad day at work?"

I looked at both of them for a moment. Why not call the bitches on it? Who was that fucker on my grass a few hours ago? I wanted to scream and point and rage and act like a raving lunatic. But I couldn't. I didn't want it to end, not just yet. And if I called them on it, they could lie. I would have to set a trap and let them fall into it.

I stared down at my plate and said, "Just tired is all."

"Well, you need your strength," Carrie said and smiled. "For later."

I just nodded. Later, my ass.

After dinner, Carrie asked me to take out the garbage. I took it outside to the garbage cans on the street. As I came back up the drive, I noticed that the trunk of Veronica's Jaguar was ajar.

I walked over and was about to slam it shut when something caught my eye. I lifted it up. Inside the trunk were four very large and very expensive suitcases.

I couldn't deny it anymore, could I? There was definitely something up. Definitely. Maybe they weren't out to kill me. That was a pretty stupid thought and the only reason I thought about it was because it was easier than thinking about them leaving. But I had to take that into consideration now. Maybe they were going to leave me. And if they left me, they might as well kill me.

· · ·

The next day, I went on the search for Arthur. I finally found him in the break room eating a Krispy Kreme donut. I grabbed his arm—he dropped the donut—and pulled him into a corner.

"What the hell is your problem, Clark?" he hissed and licked his fingers.

"You were right! They're planning on doing something!"

He was flabbergasted. "Really? I was right?"

I nodded. I decided to leave the part about the other man out. I didn't want him to know everything. Nor did I want him say anything to the effect of, "Knew you couldn't satisfy them."

"I can't believe this shit! Damn!" I kicked the trashcan. "What am I going to do?"

"What do you think they're going to do, man?"

I forced myself to say, "I think they're going to leave. Together."

He didn't miss a beat, "When are they leaving?"

I shook my head. He could have at least told me I might be wrong.

"I have no idea!" I shouted and thought about Mr.4x4. I wondered if he was at my house right then. Bastard.

"Shit, man, that sucks," he said and shook his head.

"I knew it was too good to be true! I knew it."

He said, "It always is."

"What am I going to do?"

"You should move out."

Move out?

"You know," he said. "Lay low for a while."

"And go where?" I asked. "What about Meredith's? She's my—"

"Meredith?! You've got another woman now?!"

"She's my aunt!"

"Oh," he said. "Oh."

"Tell me what to do!"

"I don't know, to tell you the truth," he said. "You have to have some proof that they're trying to do you in."

But I didn't think they were trying to do me in. I just thought they were going to leave me. The murder part was easier to admit to than the leaving part, for some reason. I didn't tell him that, though. It was none of his business anyway.

"How can I get proof?" I asked.

"Just watch them for a little while. They'll slip up."

"Then what?"

"Turn them over to the cops."

I stumbled back. The cops? That was really…definite.

"You think?" I asked.

"I know," he assured me.

The paranoia begins…

So I began to watch them. In actuality they weren't really acting all that differently. But then I noticed they began to ask me to do things…

First of all, they wanted me to fix the lamp in the bedroom. Wasn't that just great? They watched me as I did it. Why were they watching me?

"Be careful," Carrie said and smiled at me.

Veronica handed me a screwdriver, with the sharp side pointing towards me. I jumped away and held my hands up.

"What are you doing?" I screeched.

"I thought you might need it." She glanced down and noticed the way it was turned and turned it around. "Oops."

Oops, indeed.

I finished fixing the lamp and plugged it in. It blew a breaker and we were in the dark.

The next morning as I was shaving, Carrie came in, ruffled my hair and took the razor out of my hand.

She said, "Allow me."

I was actually surprised. She never wanted to shave me. But now she did? Why? What if…? That's right. Did she actually think I was going to let her shave me with that thing!? That I would just stand there and let her cut me up? I didn't think so. Well, she was doing a good job and I let her do my cheek and chin but when she got to my neck, I took the razor out of her hand.

"What is it?" she asked.

"I think I should do this part," I told her.

She shrugged and turned on the shower.

When I got home from work, they were cooking. I came in quietly and heard Carrie say, "Put some of that in. He likes that."

I watched with horror as Veronica picked up something and started to add it to the pot. I raced over and grabbed it out of her hand.

"And what is this?" I asked.

Veronica leaned over and checked the label and said, like such a smartass, "Ginger."

I stared at the label. "Appears so."

She took it back and shook her head. "*Appears so?*"

I backed out of the kitchen and said, "Carry on."

"What the hell is wrong with him?" she asked Carrie.

"He's weird, always has been," she replied.

I have not always been weird!

Instead of going to the couch and vegetating like normal, I went into the bedroom and began to look around. There were no signs of the suitcases, of course. They had to be discreet after all. So, I went to the nightstand and took a look in there. In it were their vibrators, the ten inch rubber cock and a pair of handcuffs! A pair of handcuffs and, oh dear Lord, there was a ballgag in there, too!

I knew it. They *were* up to something. And that something happened to be tying up and gagging me and torturing me and—

Carrie called, "Clark!"

"Yes?" I yelled back and waited. She didn't answer, so I yelled, "I SAID YES!"

"DINNER IS READY!" she yelled back.

"Oh," I muttered. "I bet it is."

I put the ballgag back just as Veronica tackled me and wrestled me to the bed. I tried to hold her off but sometimes she got very rowdy. And she was pretty damn strong, too.

"Hold on!" I yelled.

"What were you looking for in the nightstand?" she teased.

I glanced at the nightstand and then back at her. "Oh, nothing."

She gave me a look.

"For...some...reading material," I said.

"For the bathroom?" she said and wrinkled her nose.

"No!"

"Come on," she teased. "You still jerk off, don't you?"

I glared at her. What an absurd assumption and of course I still did it occasionally. I was a man after all!

"I do not," I huffed and crossed my arms.

"Wanna try it?" she said and leaned over and nibbled my ear. "Want me to tie you to the bed?"

"What for?"

"So I can do whatever I like to you," she said and licked my neck.

I threw her off me and hissed, "I don't think so."

She stared up at me and said, "What the fuck is your problem? Carrie loves it when I tie her up and I love it when she does it to me."

My eyes popped out. Carrie had just then come through the door drying her hands on a towel.

"Tell him Carrie."

"Tell him what?" she asked.

"How much we love being handcuffed."

"Magnificent," she said and nodded. "Want to try?"

"No, I do not," I said and left the room.

They had to be out of their minds if they thought I would let them tie me up and... Oh fucking hell! Did I just turn that down?! What kind of idiot was I? But what about the other man, Mr.4x4, and what about... Fuck Mr.4x4! He was getting his and I was going to get mine.

I went back in the bedroom. They were chattering on the bed. When I came in, they looked over at me as if they were expecting me to come back in.

"Offer still good?" I asked and loosened my tie.

They grinned and pulled me down on the bed.

"You're going to love this, Clark," Carrie told me as she handcuffed me to the bed posts.

I wasn't so sure. But then again I couldn't do anything about it now. They were already getting started. I just lay there and hoped I didn't get hurt. Too much.

They started by running their hands up and down my body. My dick got hard immediately. The nibbling started and then their hands began to go under my clothes. I was so turned on it almost hurt.

"Take your clothes off," I told them.

"We are in control," Carrie said. "Not you."

She had a point there. Not that I let that stop me.

I said, "Please. I want to see your naked bodies."

They giggled and shook their heads. Carrie unbuttoned my shirt and ripped it open. She began to kiss my chest, concentrating on my nipples. Veronica unzipped my pants. They helped each other pull my pants down and then they got on either side of me and began to lick my dick.

I groaned. This was almost too much. I wanted my hands on them so bad. I wanted to touch and rub but all I could do was lie there and try to enjoy what they were doing. And I was enjoying it—don't get me wrong—it was just so much sensation that I was headed into overload.

Carrie deepthroated me as Veronica licked my balls, taking them into her mouth. It felt so good, I almost died. Having those two heads down there at the same time was better than anything. Their hair fell over my legs and felt so soft.

"Don't let him come," Veronica told Carrie.

Carrie stopped sucking me.

Veronica came up to my mouth and began to kiss me as she kept her hand on my balls. She licked my lips and sucked on my tongue and began to moan.

That was a good sign.

I pulled back and said, "Take your clothes off."

She shook her head and grabbed Carrie and they began to kiss. Their tongues licked the other's lips as if they were tasting each other before they disappeared into their mouths.

"Come on," I said. "Take your clothes off."

"If you don't shut up," Veronica said. "I'm gonna put that gag in your mouth."

"Please."

"We mean it," Carrie said.

So I just laid there and watched as they began to press their bodies together. I watched as they began to feel each other up and I loved the way they did it, too. They didn't do it delicately; they grabbed each other's tits and asses and pushed themselves onto each other. Veronica pushed Carrie's head back and began to suck on her neck. Carrie moaned and pushed her hand down Veronica's pants. Veronica moved a little so she could get it in deeper. Carrie kept her hand there and gyrated against Veronica who was humping her hand. Veronica ran her hand up Carrie's bare leg, pushing her skirt up over her hips and rubbing her ass. She gave her a good slap and Carrie shuddered. Veronica grabbed the back of Carrie's thong and played with it, and then she slid her finger along her ass and back down to her pussy, which was swollen and wet.

"Come on," I said. "Take your clothes off."

They ignored me and kept at each other. Carrie's hand was now moving vigorously inside Veronica's pants and Veronica was about to come. She kept her hand on Carrie's pussy and did the same to her. They stayed like that until they both came, shuddering and moaning and groaning. They fell back on me and didn't move for a moment.

My dick hurt. It trembled but soon the pain was replaced by pleasure as their hands were on it again. They moved against me and began to tear their clothes off. Soon they were naked and pressing up against my naked body and their legs were on my legs and their pussies were in my face, both of them. I pressed my face into Carrie's, who let out a tiny scream. She pushed her pussy into my face as she kissed Veronica who ran her hands through my hair and tugged at it. My tongue slid along her pussy and I parted her lips with it, and then pushed it inside her. She moaned and Veronica grabbed my head hard. It was a little painful but I didn't let it bother me. I began to suck on Carrie, right on her clit until she began to hump my face and come.

As she was coming, Veronica got down and began to suck me off. She went after it, too, sucking so hard I almost burst. I began to come hard and once I did, she sucked me dry. She turned to Carrie and they kissed, sharing my cum, which slid along their mouths which they sucked and swallowed until every drop was gone.

Oh, my God.

They stopped kissing and stared into each other's eyes, licking their lips. They turned to me and bent down, each taking turns giving me kisses, back and forth they went, only stopping occasionally to give each other a kiss. We did that for a very long time until we were ready to go again.

As soon as I was hard again, Veronica grabbed the key and uncuffed me. Before I had time to rub my sore wrists, she demanded, "Slap my ass."

I slapped her ass. She shook and shivered and told me to do it again. I did it again. Carrie jumped on me and threw me down on the bed. She got on top of me and pushed my dick inside her. She began to ride me, holding onto the bedpost.

Veronica got up and left the room. I watched her go but didn't think anything about it until she came back into the room with a little riding crop.

"This was supposed to be a surprise," she said and smiled wickedly. "But I can't wait."

Carrie moaned, "Oh, yeah."

"Keep fucking him," she ordered and got behind her.

"Do it, baby," Carrie moaned.

Veronica drew back the crop and it landed on Carrie's ass with a little *smack!*

"A little harder, baby," Carrie instructed and raised her ass up more.

Veronica hit her a little harder and Carrie shuddered.

"OUI!" Carrie cried and came back down on my dick. "Now I will fuck his brains out!"

All I could do was lie there and hold on to the ride. Carrie fucked me and Veronica would occasionally slap her across the ass with the crop. She always bent down and rubbed the place where she hit and kissed it.

Once she said, "Tell me when it's too much."

"Never too much!" Carrie hissed. "Do it more, then I do you."

She gave her a few more whacks. The last one sent her over the edge. She shook, her entire body began to shake almost violently and she roared,

"AHHHHHHHOOOHH!" as she came. I grabbed her ass and pumped into her as hard as I could. The bed began to rock and we fell off it but we didn't fall apart, we kept coming and it seemed to last a long time. After we were finished we fell away from each other and just laid there panting.

I was almost worn out. But…

"My turn," Veronica said.

"You'll have to give me a minute," I said, still shocked I had lasted that long.

They eyed me and Veronica bit her lip and lit a cigarette. She took a puff, and then held it to my mouth. I inhaled, thanked her and exhaled. Phew.

After a few minutes, she bent down and began to give me head until I was hard again. She said, "Ready?"

"Ready," I said.

We got back on the bed and Veronica got on. She grabbed my face and kissed me hard before she began to move. Carrie began to swat at her ass and she came in no time. She came so hard, the whole bed was shaking. I was coming too and we began to slap against each other. It was like something just took us over and we just went with it.

"I love fucking you," she hissed as Carrie gave her another swat with the crop. "Oh, yeah! Oh, GOD! FUCK ME, CLARK!"

I fucked her until she came and I came and then it was over. I was so weak I couldn't move.

I grabbed the crop and demanded that they get on the bed with their asses turned around. They didn't hesitate. They jumped on the bed, got on hands and knees and stuck their asses out towards me.

I gave each of them a good smack, ran my hands over their asses and kissed where I'd just slapped. Their asses were a little red and as I rubbed them, they began to squirm and moan. Their legs began to part a little. I shoved them back together.

"Hold on," Carrie said and ran to the closet. She pulled out a strap on. I watched as she put it on. Wow. Where did that thing come from?

"Lie down," Carrie told Veronica.

Veronica lay down on the bed and she began to fuck her with it! Oh, my God. I couldn't move as they fucked each other with that dildo. I just stood there and watched. I found myself stroking my hard cock.

"Now you do me!" Carrie yelled at me.

Veronica rolled over, Carrie stuck it in her.

"Come here," Veronica called to me.

I raced over and she raised her ass so I could stick it in her. We fucked like that until we all came again and I like to think we came at the same time.

I have never been so satisfied in all of my life. Mr.4x4 indeed. Bet he couldn't have done just that.

Afterwards...

They were sitting on the floor sharing a cigarette. From the bed, I watched them. They looked so hot, yet innocent at the same time.

As I stared at them, I felt my heart jump. They were so great, so wonderful. And it wasn't just the sex that made me feel that way about them, it was more. They were kind women. Kind to me and to each other. Maybe I was just being paranoid about them leaving and/or killing me. They weren't capable of such things. I was just stupid. But what about Mr.4x4? How did he play into all this?

I cleared my throat and they looked over at me. I smiled at them and they smiled back.

"Tomorrow," I said, testing them. "I want to tie both of you up at the same time."

Carrie said, "Very good, darling."

Veronica laughed a little and said, "We'll have to get another set of cuffs, though."

"We can do that," Carrie said and took the cigarette out of her hand and smoked it. "I like that idea."

I liked it, too. But I was also on the verge of more paranoia. And I wanted some reassurance, so I said, "What do you girls find attractive about me?"

Again, they stared at me then they glanced at each other and shook their heads. I know, I know. I shouldn't have been so needy. But I was hoping to trip them up. Or at least get a good compliment and some sort of guarantee that this was going to last, even though my gut told me it wouldn't.

Carrie said, "Oh, Clark, you know why."

"Why?" I asked.

She glanced at Veronica and said, "Because you are handsome and do funny things."

"Really?" I asked hopefully.

She nodded. "Very much so."

Veronica agreed by saying, "You'd make good babies."

Carrie eyed her.

"Did I just say that?" she said and shook herself. "What I meant was that you're hot, Clark. So hot, in fact, that most women—if not *all* women—would want to jump your bones."

I nodded. I could see that. I suppose.

"Stop being so insecure," Carrie said.

"I'll try," I replied and closed my eyes. Before long, I drifted off to sleep. They had really worn me out. I heard something and jerked awake. I looked around and they were still on the floor talking quietly as not to disturb me. I liked that they had that much consideration.

I was about to go back to sleep when I heard Carrie said, "No, I always hated it."

I woke up in a hurry.

"Why's that?" Veronica asked and lit another cigarette.

"My mother wanted to be ballerina, but couldn't," she said. "So she made me do it for her. She pushed me and made me do it. I was good. I had the right body and the right feet and—"

"The right *feet*?" Veronica asked.

She sighed, "In ballet you must have good feet. Your arches must be good because they...ummm. For good jumps."

"Oh."

I turned on my side and watched them, keeping my head ducked so they would think I was still asleep. I couldn't help but think how odd it was that they were having this nice, tender conversation just after they had whipped one another with a riding crop and used a strap-on dildo on each other. I would never be able to figure women out. Never. Thank God.

"Yes," Carrie mumbled. "But as I said, I hated it. I cried when I was little girl because I did not want to go to class but she would force me. And when I got home, I would have to practice, practice, practice."

"So you didn't have much of a childhood?"

"No," she said and rubbed her eyes. "I did not."

"I hate that for you."

"I did not like it very much, either," she said and took the cigarette.

"What about your father?"

"My father was businessman and always away making money. What about your father?"

"I can't complain," Veronica replied. "But he was lazy and didn't work much. We were poor."

"Terrible."

"No, not really," she said and smiled. "I mean, my sister and I didn't get to do much or have many toys, but we had a big backyard and we would play for hours out there until Mom called us in for supper."

"Sounds wonderful."

"It was nice," she said and smiled up at the ceiling, as if the memory made her smile. "We grew up healthy and pretty much happy. Nothing really to complain about."

Carrie smiled sadly.

She touched her arm and said, "Tell me more."

"More?"

"More about the ballet. What happened?"

Carrie sighed and flicked the ash off the cigarette into an ashtray. "I was a very good ballerina but had no discipline. But as I say, I was good and they would let me get away with things other girls could not. I worked and worked and soon I was going to be prima ballerina."

"And then?"

"And then… And then I got an offer to come to New York to dance with their ballet."

"Sounds exciting."

"No," Carrie said and shook her head.

"No?"

"I moved to New York only to get away from my mother."

"That's terrible," she said and took her hand. "

"No, it is not terrible. I met Clark and I met you and am having a great time now."

"I feel the same way."

They smiled at each other. There was something very warm and kind and understanding in that smile.

"If I had stayed in Paris," Carrie said. "I would have been prima and very rich and famous. But I had no heart for it. I hated it. It is a hard life and the only life for a ballerina is the life of the ballet."

Veronica nodded.

"In New York, I was just another dancer and I was getting older and by then, I had no heart left for it."

"That's just so sad."

"It is," she said. "You dance to give enjoyment and pleasure to others but for yourself there is none."

"Or maybe just not for you."

"Maybe," she said and put the cigarette out. "When I arrived in New York, they loved me but I had to start at the bottom. I didn't really want to work my way up again. I was very sad."

"Why?"

"Because I lived a life for my mother and not for me," she said.

She stopped talking and stared at the wall. Veronica touched her hand and said gently, "Go on."

She sighed and said, "I was very depressed and went to a bar alone late one night."

"And?"

"I sat at the bar and drank some wine alone. I felt so bad, so bad I wanted to die."

She stopped and stared up at the ceiling and tears fell from her eyes. She had never looked so vulnerable or beautiful as she did right then. I wanted to leap from the bed and scoop her little body into my arms and hold her tight. But I wanted to hear the rest of what she had to say.

Veronica leaned over and hugged her. She allowed herself to be hugged.

Carrie continued, "And Clark came over and sat beside me. He did not say one word to me. I could not have said one word to him. But I wanted to, I really wanted to speak but I did not have the courage."

She didn't have the courage? *She?* If I hadn't been shocked, I would have been happy to hear it.

Veronica squeezed her hand. "It's okay."

"I know." Again, she gave her the same sweet smile. "Finally, I could not stand it anymore and I got up and told him to come with me. He followed and we went to his apartment and made love. He was so good, even if a little drunk and I never felt like that with another man."

Wow.

"Cool," Veronica said.

She smiled. "Yes, cool. But when I woke in the morning, I had to go back to my life. Clark did not...how do you say...fit into my schedule."

"That sucks."

"It did," she said. "And then I found out about the baby..."

"Wow."

"Yes," she said. "Sometimes a baby doesn't always come when you want it."

"Yeah."

"There's nothing you can do about it," she said. "So, I thought, it's time for a baby."

"Yeah."

"But I knew I couldn't have a baby and decided to get rid of it."

"Oh?"

"Yes," she mumbled. "I did not tell anyone and made the appointment to get rid of it. But I would not go to the appointment and it was too late and I decided I would keep it. I found Clark and told him."

"What did he say?"

"Not much at first," she said, laughing. "But then he was fine about it. Very supportive."

"I wouldn't have expected otherwise from him."

"I know," she said, still smiling. "We decided to get married. And I was about to quit the ballet when they offered me the lead in *Sleeping Beauty.*"

"Uh huh," Veronica said.

"I know I was very selfish," she muttered. "But I wanted to do it because it would be my final performance and I thought I could. I kept the baby a secret and practiced to perfect my performance."

"Yeah?"

"One day, as I was practicing…" She stopped and stared at the wall. "And…you know."

"Oh, honey," Veronica said and pulled her to her shoulder. She stroked her hair and kissed the top of her head. "I'm so sorry."

"I was sorry, too," she said. "Everything for nothing."

Veronica was now crying with her. They sat there and held each other as they cried.

She stopped for a moment and said, "But, I had Clark and was very happy."

She was happy with me?

"I know," Veronica said. "You're lucky to have him."

"I know," she said, crying. "And I was mean to him, such a bitch. It's so hard to make friends and he was my only friend and I hated him for it."

"Oh, you are not a bitch."

"But it's hard for me to make friends. People think I'm a bitch and when they see me, they run from the room."

"No they don't."

"They do," she said. "I don't…*communicate* well."

That was certainly true.

Veronica sighed. "It's just because you're so beautiful that people automatically think they can't talk to you. That's all."

"Maybe," she replied dryly. "And maybe because I am French."

"Nah," Veronica said. "It's just you're intimidated by other people and don't like to make that first move. When I met you, I had to smile at you first."

"I remember. I liked that you smiled at me."

"I enjoyed doing it."

"But when we moved here, I taught ballet but hated it still but what else could I do?"

"What do you *want* to do?" Veronica asked.

"Cook," she said. "You know, I love to cook. Maybe I could be a chef!"

What the hell!?

"Oh, you'd make a great chef," Veronica said.

"I do cook very well," she said. "I learned when I was little from our maid who would cook for us. She was very good teacher."

"You should do it!"

"What?"

"You should go to culinary school and learn to be a chef."

"Maybe I will," she said. "Maybe I will."

I closed my eyes and shook my head. Everything made so much sense to me now. Why hadn't I seen her pain? Was I that insensitive? I suppose I just thought that because she was bitchy, she hated me. But she wasn't really *that* bitchy, just outspoken. And sometimes her words came out wrong. She felt safe with me and allowed herself to be herself around me, that's all.

I shook my head again. Veronica had drawn out her deepest, darkest secrets in a matter of minutes. I hadn't been able to do that in years, though I would ask her all sorts of questions and wanted to know everything about her. She didn't divulge that much information.

But then again, maybe I hadn't asked the right questions.

"I am so glad we met," Veronica said. "I really care for you and Clark."

"I care for you to," she said. "And so does Clark."

She took her hand and said, "To me, this is not just about sex. It is about love."

"I agree," Carrie said and they touched lips and kissed. "I have never in my life felt so content and happy with anyone else. And I mean that."

"I mean it, too," she said.

They sat there and smiled at each other for a moment, then got up and left the room, saying something about leftover pizza.

Maybe Mr.4x4 had just been the pizza delivery guy.

I laid there and tried to clear my mind. I had to get this gunk out or I would be miserable forever.

Just then Carrie came back in, bent and retrieved the cigarettes from the floor and started out again. I sat up and stared at her. She caught me staring and stopped abruptly as if I'd caught her doing something. But then she smiled.

I asked her, "Is it love you feel for her?"

She sighed and considered. "Yes, for her and for you."

I nodded but didn't say anything. She studied me for a moment then sat down on the bed.

As she smoothed the hair out of my eyes, she said, "I think that love is when you know you want to be with someone and hope they are never in pain. I feel that way."

"Oh."

"And you?"

"I feel the same way."

"Very good," she said and smiled at me.

I smiled back. "I really do love you, Carrie. I really, really do."

"I know, Clark," she said softly. "And I love you."

So I guess it was love. I just never imagined it could have been so good.

Let them talk.

After that, I made the decision to just let it go. Let them all fucking talk. Let Arthur and my boss and the other people at work talk. Let Mr.4x4—whoever the fuck he was—talk. Aunt Meredith could talk. Hell, anybody could talk. And if the talk was about me, I didn't give one shit. I had a good thing, a damned good thing and I wasn't going to fuck it up.

The next morning, the girls sent me off to work with a bag of powdered doughnuts. We had slept in and didn't have time to fix breakfast.

As I was about to start eating, Arthur barged into my office and snatched the doughnut out of my hand.

"What the fucking hell!" I yelled.

"What is this?" Arthur said and peered at it. "A powdered doughnut. Ummm…"

Who the hell did he think he was? I rolled my eyes.

He sniffed it and said, "Probably covered with arsenic!"

"It came from the store!"

"Yeah, but if it's covered in arsenic, you can't detect the taste. I know their game now…slow death. See, what they do is cover it in arsenic everyday and little by little, they kill you. You're sick, but not *too* sick. *Yet.* It's a bad way to go, Clark."

"What movie did you see that in?" I asked.

He scoffed, "I didn't see it in a movie!"

"Oh."

"I read it in a book."

I shook my head and said, "The doughnut is not poisoned, Arthur."

"It's not?" he asked and sniffed it again, then he took a bite. "Yeah, you're probably right."

I got another doughnut out of the bag and said, "They're not trying to kill me, Arthur."

"They tried to kill me."

"Bullshit," I said.

He eyed me.

"You're still here, aren't you?" I asked.

"Your point being?"

"That you're paranoid and you've made me paranoid. Paranoia feeds on itself."

"But you said they had bought luggage."

"Yes, but—"

"Just don't turn your back, buddy."

"Well, whatever, but I'm perfectly content with the way things are now. They are two of the sweetest women in the world." I sighed happily. "Nothing could convince me otherwise."

He finished the doughnut and licked his fingers. "At least not until it's too late."

· · ·

After I got home, I went into the kitchen smiling. I was thinking about using the handcuffs on *them* tonight. They had agreed that we could try it sometime and sometime was now. I was going to tie them up and have my way. I also thought about using the—

What the fuck was that? I shook my head and took a closer look. Veronica was holding a box of rat poison. She was holding a box of rat poison!

What the hell?!

She was standing at the counter and oh, so casually stuffing rat poison into cheese balls! Cheese balls! I loved cheese balls! She knew that!

She looked up and smiled at me. "Hey, honey! We're—"

Nothing doing. I was outta there!

I ran all the way to my car. At first, it wouldn't start. Damned piece of shit! When it finally turned over, I drove it like a bat out of hell to the closest bar and ordered a double. Then another double and then another and then...

Yeah.

I began to tell the haggard bartender about what was going on, down to the last dirty detail, which was, of course, the rat poison. I sat there and got hammered and he listened, occasionally drying a glass or serving another customer.

"And then, I just ran out," I told him. "Why would she be stuffing rat poison into cheese balls?"

He said sarcastically, "Maybe it was for rats. Do you have any rats in your house?"

"No!" I muttered and thought about that. But then I remembered something.

A few days ago Carrie had gotten out of bed. Veronica was already in the shower. Carrie opened the closet and let out this really blood curdling scream.

I jumped up and yelled, "What is it?!"

She pointed, "SOURIS!"

"What the fuck is that?" I yelled.

"SOURIS!" she said and jumped up on the bed. "Get it now! Get it!"

I looked around wildly. What the fuck was she talking about?

I turned back to her and said, "I need some help here. What is it?"

She was still jumping and screamed, "Souris! Souris! Mice, mouse!"

She really needed to work on her English. I thought about what she had just said. A souris was a mouse? A mouse? *A MOUSE!* There was a mouse in the house? Oh, God!

Okay, calm down. What should I do? I guess I'd have to catch it. I glanced down and the damn thing ran between my feet. I yelped and jumped.

Veronica ran in and looked around wildly. "What is it?!"

"A mouse!" I yelled and pointed.

She looked around, spotted the mouse and said, "You two pussies."

She left the bedroom, came back with a broom, found the mouse and bashed its little brains in.

We watched her, half loving her for doing it and half terrified that she had. And that's why she had been stuffing rat poison into cheese balls. Just in case there were any other mice that might be around. I was a great big asshole. Well, there you go.

The bartender eyed me and nodded. "Thought so."

"Oh, shit," I muttered and rubbed my eyes. "But I m telling you, they're trying to kill me!"

He said, "Man, you've got two beautiful women in your bed and you want sympathy from me?"

"They really are. They're going to kill me!"

"Then you'll die a happy man."

After he went to the other side of the bar in disgust, I hit my head on the bar several times. I couldn't win. I should just stop trying.

One of them.

I decided to go home and face the music. I would beg for their forgiveness and maybe we could have some hot make-up sex. After that I wanted a long nap. I was tired as fuck and was feeling a little queasy, to say the least. The hot dog I picked up at the convenience store was doing somersaults in my stomach.

Maybe it was just my nerves.

The house was dark and empty looking as I approached it. Just as well. If they didn't leave me before the rat poison incident, they should afterwards.

I sighed and got out of the car, walked up the walk and into the house. Just as I was about to flip the light, I heard Carrie yell, "*SURPRISE!*" and the lights came on, blinding me.

All these people I didn't recognize smiled and cheered and shouted. In the middle of all these strangers were Veronica and Carrie, who were smiling and carrying a birthday cake towards me covered with sticks of dynamite! No, it was just those sparkly things. But it was scaring the shit out of me nonetheless.

It was my birthday? No. My birthday wasn't until next week.

I tried to smile and be thankful that someone wanted to give me a party, but then I finally just gave up.

Drunk, and exhausted, I fell to the floor and passed out. The paranoia finally won. The scotch hadn't helped matters, either.

· · ·

The dreams I had were awful. I don't remember them but they exhausted me. I moaned and rolled over. The bed felt so good but it was spinning. I thought I was going to throw up. I tried to get off the bed but could only hold on to it and pray that it would stop spinning. I heard a noise coming from beneath it. I leaned down and took a look under the bed. Nothing under there but the music was a little loud.

The music... Where was that music coming from? It was techno. I hated techno.

I shook my head and rolled back over and tried to kick the covers off but they kept coming back to cover me and try as I could, I could not push them off me.

I screamed, "NOOOO!"

I jerked awake and looked around. I focused on Carrie who stared at me pitifully. I focused on Veronica who looked on with concern. I focused on the window. It was daylight. I was in a cold sweat.

I asked, "What was going on last night?"

Carrie leaned over and pressed a wet washcloth onto my forehead. "A surprise party for your birthday."

Veronica said, "It was a good one, too. Too bad you had to miss it."

"My birthday isn't until next week," I said.

They nodded and Carrie put her arms around me.

"We wanted to surprise you," Veronica said. "With something."

"Something?"

She smiled and said softly, "We'll talk about it later. You're really tired."

I stared at her and pushed Carrie off me. I tried to get off the bed, but almost fell down. They helped me back onto it and pushed me down.

"What's wrong with me?" I asked.

"The doctor—" Veronica began.

"The doctor?" I asked.

She nodded. "One of my friends who I invited happens to be a doctor and he said you had a little food poisoning."

Food poisoning? I was suddenly aware that she had basically admitted it! They had poisoned me!

I jumped up and said, "So you admit it!"

They glanced at each other and then back at me.

Carrie said, "Admit what?"

"That you re trying to kill me!"

They yelled, "What?!"

I began to pace. "I'm on to your game! The two of you have been after me all along! You want me out so you can fly off to France with all of Veronica's money!"

They glanced at each other again and sighed simultaneously.

Veronica said, "Clark, we were going to ask you to come along. That was part of your surprise."

"My ass, surprise! Were you going to tell me before or after you killed me!"

"Before!" Carrie exclaimed. She stopped and considered. "I mean after... I mean... I don't know the word! It was a surprise!"

"Damn right it was a surprise!" I yelled. "How do you think I felt?"

"We just want to please you," she said and looked at Veronica for help.

"And what about Mr.4x4?" I demanded to know.

"What?" Carrie asked. "What is 4x4?"

"It's a truck," Veronica told her.

"Oh," she replied and stared at me. "I don't understand."

I wagged my finger in their faces. "I saw him!"

"Who?" Veronica asked.

"Mr.4x4!"

"Who is Mr.4x4!" she yelled.

"That guy," I said. "That motherfucker who was playing around with you in the front yard!"

She didn't know who the fuck I was talking about. She shook her head at me.

"He drove a black pickup?" I said. "Big, muscular guy?"

"Randy?" she asked.

So *that* was the fucker's name!

She and Carrie cracked up and they didn't stop laughing for a good minute.

"What is it!?" I yelled.

"Randy is her ex-husband, Clark," Carrie said.

Veronica nodded.

"What was he *doing* here?" I asked, crossing my arms.

They glanced at each other and Veronica said, "Bumming money."

I stared at her.

"I'm a soft touch," she said. "He's always bumming money from me."

"But you and he were getting all touchy-feely!"

"Were you spying on us?" Carrie asked.

"No!" I scoffed. "I came home one day and he was here."

"Clark," Veronica said. "We asked him to dinner so you two could meet, but he had to leave. I forgot he came."

"But you were touchy-feely!"

"We've always been," she said. "You'd think we fucked him or something."

I growled. Well, damn. Mr.4x4 was a bum. That didn't surprise me. They stared at me, trying to contain their laughter. I had to get them on something even though I didn't have shit.

"What about the rat poison?" I asked.

"For the rats?" Carrie asked and shivered. "We got rid of them."

"So it was only for the rats?" I asked suspiciously.

"Well, yeah," Veronica said.

"In cheese balls! Rat poison in cheese balls!"

She nodded. "Yeah, Clark. It's easier that way."

"But, but," I said, trying to come up with something. I gave up and said, "What else do you have to do before I get the hint that you two don't want me around?"

They sighed and shook their heads. It was a little over the top but I wanted to know for sure. I wanted them to tell me they weren't going to leave me.

"Clark you're tired," Carrie said.

"And a little delusional," Veronica added.

Maybe I was. I wasn't. Was I? What was wrong with me?

"Me?" I said. "You two are so smooth! You were just playing me until you could run off together!"

"Clark, you are tired and it appears, a little drunk," Veronica said. "Why don't you lie down and rest? We can talk about this later."

I had one last point. "I saw the luggage."

"Huh?" she asked.

"In your car. The luggage." I took a breath. "I thought you were going to leave without me."

"Why would we do that?" Carrie asked.

"No pun intended, but I am kinda like the odd man out here!"

"Clark," Carrie said. "You are insane! You think we're trying to kill you and then leave you and then... I don't know what you want!"

I didn't either.

"I give you everything and you don't even trust me!" She threw her hands up and said, "I have had enough!"

She stomped out of the room. I stared at Veronica. She stared back at me a little contemptuously.

"I am, you know?" I said.

She asked, "You're what?"

"The odd man out."

"Yeah, and you kinda screwed everything up," Veronica said before she left.

"Wait!" I ran after her and stopped her in the hall. "Where are you going?"

"Does it really matter to you? I mean, you probably wouldn't believe me if I told you." She shook her head at me. "You finally succeeded, Clark."

"What?!"

"In letting other people ruin your life."

I stared at the floor. She was right.

"I thought you were different and I guess I was wrong. You turned out to be like all the rest."

That hurt. It felt like someone had knifed me.

She paused and tears welled up in her eyes like she was so ashamed of me. "Congratulations. You've become one of those assholes you work with."

And with that, she and Carrie left.

Served me right.

I tried to find them but it was like they disappeared off the face of the earth. Served me right.

I went to work the following Monday and tried to forget about it. On Tuesday, I was walking down the hall with some files in my hand. I was staring down at the floor and didn't notice when Dave dropped in step beside me.

"Hey, Clark!" he exclaimed and slapped me on the back. "Heard your old lady, or shall we say, *ladies*, kicked you out."

Yeah, I thought gloomily, all because of people like you.

"News certainly travels fast around here, doesn't it?" I said.

He gave me a real shit eating grin. "It sure does!"

I stopped, stared him dead in the eye and gave him a very menacing look. "Do you know what your fucking problem is?"

He seemed taken aback. "What?"

"You're too fucking nosey!" I hissed. "Why don't you get a life and stay out of mine?"

I took off without another word. If that bastard said another word to me again, I was going to kick the shit out of him.

I stomped back into my office, threw the files down and left. I was taking the rest of the day off. Fuck these motherfuckers! I went back to the bar where I had spilled my guts. The same bartender was there. I told him what happened.

"Those are the breaks," he told me as he smoked. "Can't say that I feel sorry for you."

"I didn't expect you to," I told him and took a drag off my cigarette.

"You fucked up a good thing," he replied, nodding.

"But if something is too good to be true, then it probably is. Right?"

"Who taught you that?"

"Well, no one," I said. "It's just something everyone says."

"Yeah, just like they say money can't buy happiness," he said. "Bet the same people who say that have never worked at McDonald's."

He was right about that.

He added, "Or in a bar."

"Point taken," I said and held up my glass.

Point definitely taken.

I was passed out on the couch when the phone rang later that night. It was Veronica. She wanted to come over and see me.

"Of course, you can," I said. "I'll be waiting."

She got there about an hour later.

"How's Carrie?" I asked as soon as she sat down on the couch.

She smiled and said, "She refused to come. She's still mad at you."

"I understand," I told her. "How have you been?"

"Can't complain," she said. "Though that doesn't stop me."

I chuckled.

"How have you been?" she asked.

"Terrible."

She nodded. "I came here to ask you something. And you have to be completely honest with me."

Oh, shit.

"What is it?" I asked.

She took a breath and said, "What do you want, Clark?"

I couldn't help but smile and hope that what I wanted, I would be able to have. If they gave me a second chance, I would be the luckiest bastard on the planet.

"I just want my life back," I said excitedly. "My wife. I just want things to be like they were."

Her face seemed to go a little pale. I don't know why. Before I could ask, she said, "Okay."

"Really?" I asked.

She nodded and smiled. "Carrie's out in the car."

I grabbed her face and gave her a big kiss then ran outside. Sure enough Carrie was in the car. And she was glad to see me.

I awoke the next morning feeling like a million bucks. I hadn't screwed up as nearly as bad as I had originally thought. Which was good, to say the least.

I sighed with satisfaction recalling all the sex we had last night. It had been good. No better than good. It had been excellent.

I rolled over and snuggled against Carrie who murmured in her sleep. I looked over her to see an empty spot where Veronica usually slept. I fell back and sighed. She was probably already up. She sometimes got up a lot earlier than we did.

I got up a few minutes later and went into the kitchen to make some coffee. I didn't see her in the bathroom or in the living room or... I didn't see her anywhere. I started to call out to her but something made me go to the window instead. I looked out and noticed her car was gone. Where it usually sat was a brand new Mercedes. Then I remembered that today was my birthday.

Uh oh.

I looked around frantically and finally saw the note lying on the coffee table. It was under a small gift. I decided to open the gift first. It was the keys to the Mercedes with a little note: "Enjoy!" I went to the note.

All it said was:

> "C&C,
> All I can say is merci beaucoup.
> V."

Carrie took it out of my hand. I watched as she read it. After she finished, she fell back on the couch and put her head in her hands and began to cry. Her little body began to shake with sobs. After a minute or so, she looked up at me with tears streaming down her cheeks. God, I felt so bad. I felt like pure shit for being so small-minded. I had ruined it all.

"You son of a bitch," she cried. "What did you do to her?"

I shrugged. "I don't know. She asked what I wanted and I said…"

Oh, shit. I had said I wanted my life and my wife back and hadn't even mentioned her. I was such an asshole.

"You asshole," she spat. "You told her to leave, didn't you?"

I dropped my head and muttered, "Not in those words."

"You bastard!"

"I didn't mean it like that!" I shouted. "I didn't mean to… It came out wrong!"

She pointed at me. "Everything with you is wrong. Everything."

That hurt so bad.

"You can't love," she said. "You get insecure and jealous for no reason. You don't let it happen."

"Carrie, I didn't mean to do it."

"But you did it," she said. "It makes no difference."

"Why did she buy us a car?" I asked.

"Because our car was shit! That's why! She knew how much trouble it caused and she wanted to do something nice!"

Oh.

"She bought that car for your birthday," she cried. "You asshole. She wanted you to have it because she loved you but you love no one but yourself!"

"That's not true!" I said, on the verge of tears myself. I had really screwed this one up. I couldn't win. I was just an asshole. I screwed everything up and I didn't even try to.

She jumped up and ran into the bedroom and began to pack.

"Where are you going?" I asked, wanting to stop her but knowing there was no way I could.

"I am going to find her," she said and pointed at me. "And don't try to stop me."

I didn't. When she was finished packing, she took the keys to the new car. I don't know where she went. I don't know where Veronica went. I don't know if they found each other. All I know was that I was the world's biggest asshole.

And this is how the story ended for our hero.

The moral of the story? When you got a good thing, make it last. And don't be stupid like I was.

I had every man's dream. I had it made. They were gorgeous women and they made me laugh. They cooked me good food and all I had to do was show up. But how was I supposed to know they weren't going to leave me?

I could have used my brain, for starters. I could have stopped listening to other people. I could have enjoyed what I had instead of turning it into something ugly and messy. I could have sat back and patted myself on the back for being "the man". But I couldn't. I don't know where that insecurity came from. Maybe it was in me the whole time and the intensity of the situation just brought it out. But I could have dealt with it better. I could have…

I could have been a better man.

I learned my lesson. If I ever got another chance like that… Well, that wasn't going to happen. It was once in a lifetime thing. I just hoped that whatever man's lap it landed in next time could do it better than I did.

I was lonely at first without them. I was sure they were in Paris, France living it up. And you know what? I hoped they were. They deserved to be happy. I didn't. I had really screwed up and I got what I deserved in the end.

It was a few months later and I was just about to get my life turned around when I heard a knock on the door. As I opened it, my heart leapt into my throat. It was Veronica and Carrie. They were standing on the door step, each dressed in black outfits and looking so delicious I could have eaten them up. They looked the same, yet they were so chic and sophisticated looking. I hadn't noticed that about them before.

I was so happy to see them that I could have cried. I didn't have time to.

"Bonjour, Clark," Carrie said.

"Hey, buddy," Veronica said.

I looked at Carrie, then at Veronica and back and forth between them a few times. It was really them! They were really here! Alive and in the flesh. And that flesh looked so good.

"Hi," I said and began to shake with excitement. "What are you…? I mean… You girls look great! Wow! So—"

They held up their hands for me to be quiet and at the same time, they said, "We're pregnant."

To be perfectly honest, it didn't sink in for a moment, so I stood there feeling happy that they were standing in front of me. Then it sank in. They were back but for an entirely different reason than I had expected. I absorbed the information and the enormity of their news. I was happy at first but then it hit me like a ton of bricks. I willed myself to stay calm and to make sure I didn't act like an asshole. I passed out anyway.

And that's how it ended.

Printed in the United States
1175400001B/82